Chapter 1:

"It's been a hard day's night..." –The Beatles, Hard Day's Night

Oh no.

Not again.

This cannot be happening.

No. No. No.

I cannot go through this again. It nearly destroyed me last time.

But I don't have a choice.

I have to face it.

But not alone.

I pull out my phone and send a text.

"Tannunbum family dinner 2nite…if its tofu again somebody dies."

Family meals are interesting at my house.

Luckily for me, they don't happen very often. With all of us on different schedules, it's really hard to get all four Tannunbums in the house at the same time. Usually we just eat supper on our own. But every once in a while Mom will decide we need "quality family time" after being guilt-tripped by a Dr. Phil episode, and we sit down to eat together. Of course, "eat" implies we actually consume food. Not so much. Mom always serves a new low-fat, low-calorie and generally low-taste recipe that she and my sister will barely touch anyway. Dad and I will also barely touch it, but that's because it tastes like a health food store has vomited on our fine china. Then, after a conversation that rarely involves me, we part ways –my father and I to our secret stashes of real food and my mother and Lana to our home gym.

Unfortunately, Mom got home from shopping early enough today to hear a certain bald talk show host preaching about fractured families, so she's in the kitchen making tonight's Tannunbum Family Meal. I'm not sure what she's whipping up, but the unmistakable scent of gross wafting in isn't exactly inspiring confidence.

My phone buzzes at me. Katie is responding to my text.

"that blows girl…got any ways 2 get out of it?"

"None. Well…faking my own death=not an ok option?"

"Probs not…"

Suddenly my mother's incredibly shrill voice pierces my ears.

"Dinner is served!"

She's just walked out of the kitchen, her "Kiss Me, I'm the Cook" apron tied impossibly tight around her waist and her oven-mitted hands holding a dish high. She sets it down on the table and calls out for Dad and Lana to come downstairs.

I pull out my earbuds and hit pause on Paul McCartney and John Lennon's harmony fest. I'd love to leave them in –they'd at least provide some distraction –but Mom is clear: no iPods or phones at the table. I can't hide my texting either –I'm too slow and my parents notice me looking down for suspiciously long periods of time. Looks like I'll be going it alone. Heaving a heavy sigh, I prepare myself for the onslaught of mental anguish that is a Tannunbum family dinner. Ready to face the meal, I glance down at the crock-pot and gag on sight.

Looking as far as I can away from the crock-pot, I ask, "Um…what is this?"

"It's Risotto with salmon chunks."

At the word chunks, I gag again. This risotto looks like the contents of the trash can of someone with food poisoning. Really, really bad food poisoning.

I get up to leave.

"Morgan, where are you going?" my mother asks pointedly. "Dinner is ready."

"I'm going to wash my hands," I respond, walking away.

"And dry heave," I whisper under my breath.

"What?"

"And dry them," I say, louder. "I hate it when the fork gets all slippery."

"Oh," she laughs. "Me, too."

Please. When was the last time my mother actually used a fork?

You see, my mother is Macy Tannunbum, formerly Macy Sharon, one of the most successful Victoria's Secret Angels ever. That poster of her in a bathing suit is one of the most sold pieces of paper on the face of the planet. There are more copies of that floating around than there are of the Constitution, the Bill of Rights, and Snooki's autobiography -

combined. Many of those copies hang over the beds of my male friends who don't realize she's my mom, which is even more awkward than you'd think it is. She was 102 pounds when she got her first contract, and, other than her pregnancies, she's never really weighed much more. (And, yes Mom, it is so nice of you to remind me of that fact so often. It's so very helpful over here in the land of people who actually eat.)

My sister Lana has just walked by and is headed straight into the Land of the Risotto. She is long and lean and proportioned perfectly, having inherited all of Mom's beauty and then some. She is the subject of the other poster often hanging in my friends' rooms, although it's a lot tamer and is from *Sweet Caroline*, the Disney sitcom that launched her career. My friends don't know she's my sister, either, for the same reason they don't know my mom and I are related: we look nothing alike. Lana went straight from cute little kid to stunning teenager. She never had an awkward stage. I've never left mine.

She's three years older than me at 19, and she only lives with us because she's never bothered to leave. That's alright with me. You'd think I'd hate her –she's ridiculously pretty and is a giant success. Next to her People's Choice Awards on the fireplace mantel are my participation certificates from when my parents were still trying to force me to play organized sports. But Lana isn't a big star to me –she's my sister, the one who sometimes farts when she's nervous and used to read me stories before bed, back when we shared a room.

I've stalled as long as I can washing my hands. I would have gone all the way to my own bathroom, but Mom would've called me on it. I swear, she times my pee breaks. I've easily passed two minutes, which is cutting it close. It's time to go face the risotto, whether it bears an uncanny resemblance to puke or not. As I'm drying my hands on a towel, there's a knock on the door.

"I'm coming!" I shout.

The door opens. It's my Dad, holding a massive stack of papers.

"I'm coming," I repeat, stepping toward him.

"Oh," he said. "I just wanted to see if it was open."

Great. He's going to read whatever that is in the bathroom. He is such a guy, it's disgusting.

He sees me glancing at the giant pile in his hand. "It's a script."

"Oh, ok." I really don't care. Dad is a producer, director and writer, and he gets new scripts all the time. He'll probably talk about it nonstop at dinner tonight. Great. Almost all of Dad's films are teen-targeted, and he'll go on and on about how this shows the life of a teenager today and how Lana is a perfect fit for the lead role. Blah, blah, blah.

On the way toward the stairs, I get another text from Katie.

"good luck girl…im glad im not there anymore!!"

Katie used to be (and still pretty much is) my best friend, before she left Marquette and the greater LA area for cold, blistery Chicago with her lawyer father and art critic mother a few months ago. I miss her like crazy. She used to make me macaroni and cheese and sneak it over to my house on Tannunbum family dinner nights, hiding it in the bottom of her backpack as she and I went upstairs to "study". Now I'm stuck by myself. Ugh.

After running and putting my phone in my room, I head into the kitchen, telling Mom and Lana that Dad will be right down. I almost hope he will be. The only conversation that's more awful to tune out than Dad talking about his scripts is hearing Lana and Mom obsess over the calories they are about to ingest.

I reluctantly serve myself some risotto, looking as far away from my plate as possible. I also grab an apple and a little bit of cottage cheese. Maybe if I eat everything else on my plate, Mom won't notice that I haven't touched the risotto. She and Lana also take the serving dish, though they both look like they actually want to eat it.

After a few minutes of awkward silence, Dad comes downstairs, script in hand. What did I tell you?

He serves himself a bit of risotto and sits, plunking the packet down between him and Lana. It's fairly thick, but it's a screenplay –they're always thick.

Mom takes a moment to stop thinking about all the running she'll have to do to burn off this meal and asks, "What's this?"

"It's a new script, fresh from Avery."

Avery is my father's agent. He gets hundreds of scripts and sends the good ones on to Dad.

"It doesn't have a title…"

"No, Avery hated the original title. He scratched it and said we'd come up with a new one later."

Many writers, including my dad, cannot name their own work to save their souls. For about the first six months of development, the working title for *Sweet Caroline* was "Girl Whose Life Is Really Easy But She Still Has Some Problems." I kid you not.

"Lana, how are you liking it?" he asks, turning to my sister.

"Oh," she says, looking up. "It's really good. I'm almost done."

She and Dad go on to describe the plot: awkward girl feels like she doesn't belong in her family or have any talents to contribute. I could have told you that without ever looking at the script. All of these screenplays follow the same formula: our awkward but lovable protagonist (who is played by an actress or actor who is never very awkward looking) feels unwanted and their sibling is constantly outshining them. Then comes the interesting twist that causes a big family fight, like the parents are CIA operatives or the sibling is secretly a cocaine addict. In fixing the problem, our awkward hero or heroine, who always gets a way-too-attractive love interest, finds his or her true calling and they all get back together to sit down for a family meal before the credits roll. The end. They're so predicable that I don't even need Dad to tell me the last half of the movie. I've got it down.

"Lana, I think you'd be fabulous as Meagan."

I'm assuming Meagan's the lead role.

"I really don't think I'm what you want for the lead," Lana says.

Told you.

Actually, this comes as a surprise. Lana almost always jumps at the chance to audition for a lead. In all fairness, who wouldn't? It's a Michael Tannunbum production, which means it'll be a moderate box office success at the very least and it'll get Lana lots of exposure. Maybe she's considering a more dramatic role, the kind that will get her noticed as an adult actress. She's been talking about that a lot lately.

"May I be excused?" I ask. I've done a fairly good job of moving the risotto around, so it looks like I've actually consumed some. I've also handed several spoonfuls down to Ringo, my pug, who eagerly ate it for me. There are some benefits to not being paid attention to at the table.

Mom glances at my plate. "Yes," she says.

As soon as the words are out of her mouth, I get up from the table and take my dish to the kitchen, quickly rinsing it while trying to avoid getting any of that disgusting risotto on my fingers. I throw my plate into the dishwasher and head up to my room.

I go straight to my bookshelf and stand there pondering which titles to pull out. Even though the last time either of my parents were in my room was when I was a middle-schooler, I still take care to hide my junk food well. I've hidden most of my stash in hollowed-out books like these, many of them titles I read and then hated so much I actually enjoyed attacking them with an exacto-knife. (Seriously Herman Melville? A thousand pages about a freaking whale?) I decide on *Twilight*, home to my Reese's, and *Pride and Prejudice*, which holds my Twizzlers. I pull down *Moby Dick* for good measure, opening the atrociously thick volume to reveal my favorite junk food of all– Cheese-its. I bought the large-print edition at a thrift store, and it's actually big enough to hold an entire box.

As soon as I tear open the bag, I hear Ringo running up the stairs, right on cue. Ringo loves Cheese-its just as much as I do, if not more. I swear he's psychic –he'll run from anywhere in the house when the smell of processed cheese crackers is unleashed.

I stand up to open my door. I keep it locked at all times. Like I said, my parents haven't been in here in a while, and I'd like to keep it that way. As soon as my hand touches the knob, Ringo comes flying in, running over to the box and curling up into a ball next to it. It's his way of saying, "I love you! Now feed me."

I oblige, and I give him two or three of the crackers out of the handful I'm eating. I feel pretty bad for making him eat the risotto, even though he probably loved it. Just in case he didn't, I place four more of the little orange squares in my hand and hold them out to him. He responds by eating them all and crawling into my lap, letting his little head rest on my thigh.

I sit there scratching his ears for a while, using my other hand to eat my real food out of my fake books. Ringo is shedding all over my jeans, but I really don't care. That's part of the reason I named him Ringo in the first place –he's got long hair and he runs around like he's stoned half the time.

I think I'm finally full, although most of the Cheese-its are gone. This whole junk-food sneaking deal has gotten a lot easier since I got my license a couple of months ago, though, and it shouldn't be too difficult to pick up another box. Glancing down at my watch, I see I have an hour or so before I need to leave for Speech practice anyway, so no one will wonder why I left. I have my own car, but my parents are incessantly on my case about where I am going and who I am going with and what I will say when I am offered The Dangerous Drug Kids Today Are Doing. (I don't actually know what that is…I generally rely on Brian Williams to tell me the latest in teenage substance-related stupidity.) I gently push Ringo off my lap and start putting the Twizzlers back into *Pride and Prejudice* when…

"Damn!" I say, a little too loudly. I've managed to give myself a pretty deep paper cut on one of the edges I carved inside the book. My finger is bleeding like crazy, and the tissue I've grabbed and wrapped around it is already a dark shade of red. Mumbling a few other four-letter words, I snatch a handful of tissues and take a few steps into my bathroom, only to realize I used up all of my band-aids when I tried to shave the other day. Calling up a few more expletives, I head to the family bathroom.

Since both of my hands are focused on stopping my finger from hemorrhaging, I use my shoulder to open the bathroom door. There's no one inside, but Dad has clearly come back to keep going on his new script –the toilet seat is up and the stack of paper is on the counter. Ew.

I turn on the faucet with my elbow and run cold water over my finger, which still hurts but seems to be done bleeding. With all the blood gone, I can see the damage I've done: a nice diagonal line that's at least an inch and a half long. Great. I reach down to the bottom drawer and pull out a band-aid. As I stand up, I turn around and knock Dad's script off the counter, scattering the papers on the tile floor. Throwing out the few curse words I haven't used in the last five minutes, I wrap the band-aid around my finger and kneel to the ground, trying to pick up the papers.

As I'm trying to collect them, something stops me cold. On the second page, I see the following:

"Original Title: Scrambled Eggs."

Shit.

Chapter 2:

"Yesterday/Love was such an easy game to play/now I need a place to hide away/oh I believe/in yesterday…" –The Beatles, Yesterday

"What the hell did you do?"

I come barreling into Mrs. Kay's classroom, blowing past the door and nailing my thigh on a desk. As soon as I saw the original title of the manuscript in my bathroom, I tore through the rest of the pages as fast as I could in disbelief. Confirming my worst fears, I gathered it up, threw it in my backpack and ran out the door. The original title had put everything together for me –and what came together was not good.

"What?" She rises from her swivel chair.

I steamroll on, ignoring the throbbing in my leg and throwing the copy of *Scrambled Eggs* onto her desk. "How the hell did my dad get a hold of this?"

"You left your computer on?" She looks lost.

"No!" I practically scream. "No! It got sent to my house, by my Dad's agent, as a script for him to read!"

"What?"

"You were the only one I gave a copy to. The only one. How could you do this to me?"

She has returned to her seat and is sitting there quietly, not moving, with her eyes straight in mine. She is listening intently, something that I usually find comforting. Suddenly, however, it's infuriating, and I rage on.

"Like, what the hell? You knew that this was not supposed to be read by anyone, that I poured my soul into those two hundred pages, that the "For Your Eyes Only" written in giant red Sharpie on the envelope was not a suggestion!"

My angry speech I had planned so well on the drive over has, at this point, become one painful run-on sentence. How could she have done this to me? Mrs. Kay is the only one who has read my writing –my real writing, not the crap I show my dad to get him off my case. She was the one who gave me the courage to write *Scrambled Eggs*.

Did she just use me to make a profit? I feel tears rising, but I shove them down with one final jab.

"Just butt out, ok? I don't need you to try to fix things, or make it better, or any of that touchy-feely crap. That story, that book, that screenplay, whatever-it's *mine*, ok? *Mine*. My story. My side. For once, I was the one in charge and…"

My voice fades to silence as I realize what Mrs. Kay is pulling out of her bottom drawer, her "important drawer" that holds her first edition of *To Kill A Mockingbird* and the Dove chocolate stash Mr. Kay doesn't know about. Her bony hands are holding a thick manila envelope, and as she pulls it out a flash of red becomes visible underneath her nearly translucent skin.

She slowly sets the heavy packet down on her desk.

"Sweetie," she says. "It never left."

"Wow," Mrs. Kay says. It's probably the only word she can think of.

It's been twenty minutes since I came running through her door like a banshee, and this is the first time she's spoken, other than the occasional "Right" or "Uh-uh." After a few moments of horrified silence upon realizing I had just gone totally nuts on my only confidant, the words just fell out.

I had known she would be at school because she's the speech coach. Fortunately, she has managed to get some of the seniors to lead practice for the freshmen, and almost everybody else is far enough into the season to know what they're doing. It's just me and her –and her Dove chocolates.

"Could he have gotten it off your computer?"

"No," I say. I've already ruled that one out. Believe me, I've run every possible scenario forward, backward and probably sideways. I have no idea how my manuscript – the one that I didn't tell anybody, not even Katie, I was writing –ended up in my father's hands.

Because I sure didn't give it to him. Dad really wanted me to be a writer, always pushing me to do contests and journal my thoughts. For years, I ignored him. In case you haven't noticed, everything I do gets compared to my family. The third space on our fireplace mantel is occupied by my dad's writing Emmys. I was not going to compete with that, so I just didn't write, plain and simple. I read, which probably helped, but I never wrote my own thoughts down beyond the required school assignments. Sure, it sucked being a permanent background fixture in my own family, but I had Katie to bounce off of and things weren't too bad so long as I stayed out of the Tannunbum house. But after she moved to Chicago, I didn't have anything else to cling to. I've made a couple of new friends, but nothing compared to Katie, and I guess I finally exploded. I saw Dad ignoring all of us to focus on work and mom pushing her massive food issues straight onto Lana and me just being left in the dust and I lost it. I ran up to my room and started typing on Laverne, my laptop. (Shirley is my printer.) I just typed and typed and typed until my eyes wouldn't stay open anymore. I woke up the next morning with my head on the keys, only to realize what I'd written the night before was actually ok. More than ok, it was good. It was better than what most of the kids in my English class came up with, anyway. And so I kept going, firing up Laverne every time Mom made a comment about Lana's jeans getting to be too tight and every time my needs came dead last to everybody else's –again.

Eventually, my angry rantings became one coherent manuscript. I wrote a screenplay because, don't you dare tell my father this, I like movies. I like the magic, how the words literally leap off the page and become a picture in front of you. I eventually ended up calling it *Scrambled Eggs*, even if only out of desperation to come up with a title. That thing with authors sucking at naming their work? Apparently that applies to me, too. For those of you who aren't Beatles fans, "Scrambled Eggs" was the name for Paul McCartney's hit break-up song "Yesterday" when he had the tune worked out but couldn't come up with lyrics. It was just there to hold the place of the words until he came up with the right ones. That's how it worked with my title, too. It was just there until I came across something better. I never did, and I just never changed it.

This is why I'm utterly and completely screwed. I really wasn't planning on letting anybody read it, and so I didn't sugar-coat anything. I wrote it mostly when I was angry, which I'm sure didn't help, and the end product is a truthful but not very flattering portrait of my family. Combine that with the fact that a bunch of the anecdotes in *Scrambled Eggs* come straight from the Tannunbum family household and I am basically a sitting duck. It's a good thing my dad isn't home very often, physically or mentally, or he'd already have me figured out. Thinking that my screenplay would never leave Laverne, I didn't try very hard to conceal the identity of my characters, either. The *Scrambled Eggs* version of Dad is named Mitchell Tatum, while the narrator is Meagan verses my Morgan. The only big change is Lana: in the manuscript she's a straight-A UCLA med-schooler. The real Lana is deathly afraid of vomit and would have passed out at my paper cut earlier. But she's still named Laura, and she's almost exactly the same, raging food issues and all.

This is yet another reason I am totally dead meat. My parents can't know that I'm the author of *Scrambled Eggs*, because then they'll know that they are the subjects of it. My pseudonym, Penny Lane, won't hold up for long, and if Dad wants to make the movie, he'll need the author's permission. My permission. And I still don't know how it got off Laverne and into Avery's hands. I double-checked Laverne before I left –my passwords were all intact.

"And so that's why you came running in here," Mrs. Kay finishes for me.

"Yeah," I say.

"I wish I could help," Mrs. Kay says. "But I haven't given it to anybody to read."

That's not surprising. I should have known she'd keep her word. Besides, now that it's out I can see the handwritten notes I scrawled in the margins of nearly every page. Dad's copy was blank. Mrs. Kay didn't do it. So who did?

"But," she continues. "I can see why this Avery person passed it on to your dad. Morgan, this is good. Really good."

I shrug sheepishly. Ever since I was in her class freshman year, Mrs. Kay has been trying to convince me I'm a talented writer. I'm not so sure. I mean, I can outwrite most of my English class, but that doesn't mean much. I had to explain to someone yesterday that I didn't make up the word "senile", and no, it was not a sex joke.

"Now," she says. "Here's what you're going to do. You're probably not going to be able to focus through Musical Theater, right?"

She's right. Even though my role actually requires me to sing like crap –which is good, because that's the only way I know how to sing –trying to give a good performance is the last thing on my mind right now.

Noting my silence, Mrs. Kay moves on. "So, you go home and just breathe, ok? Everything's going to be fine."

"Home is the last place I want to be."

"Right," she says. Glancing upwards, she says suddenly in a forced whisper, "Get down, get down, get down, get down," pointing toward the trash can.

"What?"

"Stick your head in there!"

"Why?"

As soon as I hear the voice coming from the doorway, I understand Mrs. Kay's reasoning, and I shove my face into the lining of the trash can.

"Morgan, are you coming?" Sierra Solomon says, her already bratty voice singed with annoyance. Sierra is one of those girls who will "forget" to remove the $500 price tag from her designer jeans just to accentuate the fact she thinks that she's better than you. One time freshman year I thought she left it on by accident and offered her scissors. She responded by patting me on the head and explaining the purpose of leaving the tag in place. I've been in kiddy pools less shallow. "Oh," she says, I'm assuming as she sees my face plant into Mrs. Kay's trash can. "So…"

"Morgan isn't feeling very well," Mrs. Kay enters smoothly.

I throw in a few gagging noises. You know. For effect.

"It's probably the flu," she adds.

"I'm fine," I say weakly before returning my mouth to the trash can and making a few more vomiting sounds.

"So, I'll be staying with her for a while," Mrs. Kay says. "Please make sure the freshmen are on task."

"Fine," Sierra says, before the door slams.

"You're safe," Mrs. Kay says. "I don't think she'll be back."

"Thanks," I say, straightening my neck and seeing Mrs. Kay instead of the Cheeteos wrapper she threw away after lunch today.

"No problem," she replies. "You know, that was pretty convincing. Use that for an improv sometime."

Group Improvisation is my other event for the FDR High Fighting Squirrels Varsity Speech Team. (I know. It's a terrible mascot. Our opponents regularly bring signs concerning our inability to find our nuts.) I only did musical theater for the fun of showing off my atrocious vocals. All of us Tannunbums are certified tone deaf, even Lana. (Of course, that didn't stop her from being one of Disney's top-selling artists. Oh, what would the world do without autotune?) I like acting, but Lana loves it, and she can pull off anything. She even made a convincing crackhead for a Lifetime movie. Of course, if Dad has his way, she'll end up with her most difficult role ever –me.

"Morgan…Morgan!" Mrs. Kay snaps me out of my reverie.

"Yeah?"

"You," she says, pulling out her Dove chocolates and her trash can, "Can stay in here as long as you'd like. If anyone asks, pull that little food poisoning routine, ok?"

"Ok. I'm sorry, Mrs. Kay."

"For what?"

I look at her incredulously. "Oh, the plethora of four-letter words, the accusations of theft, taking you away from Speech practice…You know. Little stuff."

She laughs. "It's fine," she says. "It's a pretty understandable reaction."

"That doesn't stop me from feeling bad!"

"Well, don't," she says. "And Morgan?"

I glance up at her.

"Everything will work out fine."

It's great advice.

If only I believed it.

Chapter 3:

"The sun is up/the sky is blue/it's beautiful/and so are you." –The Beatles, Dear Prudence

After apologizing again for going crazy on her, I finally left Mrs. Kay's room at 8:30, half an hour after I would have left on a normal night. I was hoping some inspiration would hit me, but I've still got nothing, even though it's now almost two in the morning.

The burning question: What do I do now?

I have no idea what my next move should be. I could try to convince Dad that *Scrambled Eggs* is a piece of crap, but even he will probably get suspicious. Usually I couldn't care less about his scripts. I could try to get rid of the only copy he has, which he hopefully hasn't noticed has been M.I.A. for the last several hours. That's a band-aid solution, though: it doesn't solve anything, it just buys me some time. Then again, time is good. But if I destroy it, I need to destroy it in an incredibly believable way. Maybe Ringo will eat it if I put Cheese-its between the pages…that dog will do anything for a processed cheese snack….

Then, of course, there is the extremely unlikely but very terrifying possibility that Dad knows it's mine. I can so see him doing that, too, just letting me panic as he sits there smugly. If that's the case, he probably doesn't even like it, he just wants to see me sweat. Jerk.

I have zero options here, and I still have no idea how my script got off my password-protected computer and into the hands of an agent. Not just any agent, either, my Dad's agent. Granted, Dad is one of the higher-profile writer/directors in L.A. right now, especially for scripts like mine, but still: there are dozens if not hundreds of agents with connections to directors –why just Avery?

My blood runs cold as I think of another, even-worse-case scenario. What if it's not just Avery? What if my mysterious, script-sending friend (more like enemy) sent *Scrambled Eggs* to other filmmakers, too? You can't exactly look up Avery's address in the phone book. If they managed to get it to him, who else ended up with it?

I jump out of bed and fire up Laverne, waiting impatiently for my browser to open. I type "Scrambled Eggs" into Google and hit enter. I get 300,000 hits, but all of them appear to be either food or Beatles related. Just in case, I also try my name, Meagan Tatum and a few of the other main characters, all of which turn up nothing. I'm safe, I think –for now.

I breathe a sigh of relief and throw myself back down on my bed, almost hitting Ringo, who fell asleep hours ago. His snores come at a rhythmic pace. I'm so used to them I barely hear them anymore.

Suddenly, I jump at the sound of a knock at the door. I relax after I hear four taps, one long, one short, one long, one short. It's the secret code Lana and I invented when we were little.

I go over to unlock the door. I swing it open and sure enough, there's my sister, clad in an oversized Habitat for Humanity T-shirt and her favorite Minnie Mouse pajamas.

"Hey," she says, walking inside my room and plopping down on my bed. "Couldn't sleep, huh?"

"I'm a little stressed," I say. "School."

I wish I could tell her the truth. I want to tell her the truth. But I won't, and I don't for now. I need to know what I'm up against before I drag my sister into it.

"Come here," she says, backing up on the bed. I sit down, and she begins massaging my back with her bony fingers.

As soon as she touches my spine, I make a moan worthy of a porn soundtrack. (Or at least, what the guys on *Whose Line* do to make fun of a porn soundtrack.) Lana giggles behind me. She's amazing at massages, and she can always find the spots where I'm most tense.

My back, which had been straight as an arrow, has collapsed into a curved mess underneath Lana's skilled hands. After seven straight hours of nonstop adrenaline, I've pretty much melted into a puddle.

"Tired?" she asks, working her way down my spine.

"Yeah," I say. "How do you do that?"

"Do what?"

"Make me so relaxed?"

"I don't know," she says, moving back to my neck. "It's a gift, I guess."

Actually, it probably has a lot more to do with the years we shared a bedroom, until I was six and she was nine. These late nights were the norm for her even then. She tossed and turned, violently enough to sometimes fall out of bed. That meant she got the bottom bunk, which meant I shook four feet above her with every position change. (This was extremely helpful on the first and only cruise my family ever went on, as I was the only Tannunbum not incapacitated by nausea. Hah!) We'd stay up reading books out loud, braiding each other's hair, and discussing the sisterly things that can only be understood by sisters.

Once we moved into the new house, Lana and I got separate rooms, and I went back to being out cold as soon as my head hit the pillow. But my sister didn't sleep. She tried everything –audiobooks, white noise machines, pure silence. She even gave a valiant attempt at counting sheep once. She came into my room at three in the morning crying because she'd lost track somewhere in the hundred thousands. Things got worse when *Sweet Caroline* went on the air, and now my sister sleeps at most three hours a night. I really don't know what she does with all that time…

My train of thought all but stops when Lana moves on to my shoulders, sending shivers down my spine. Somehow I've gone from incredibly wired to barely conscious, and the only things that seem to be holding me up are Lana's bony hands.

"Ready for bed?" she asks, sensing my rapid descent into exhaustion.

I nod, trying to keep my eyes open.

"Ok," she says, standing up from behind me. "Sweet dreams, sis."

"Sweet dreams," I say.

I awake to find my alarm blaring, my mother pounding at my door, and Ringo crouching over my dirty laundry in a pose he usually saves for fire hydrants.

"Morgan Kate Tannunbum! Get up! It's 7:30!"

Crap.

I throw on a t-shirt and jeans, fueled by adrenaline. Putting Ringo outside after making sure he hasn't actually relieved himself on my dirty clothes, I slide on my tennis shoes and run out the door, stopping only to make sure Dad's copy of *Scrambled Eggs* lands back in the bathroom where it belongs.

I drive like a manic to school, and I slide into Pre-Calc three minutes before the bell rings. Safe!

I'm on autopilot through class, pretending to pay attention to the incredibly fascinating process that is translating a sinusoidal equation. As soon as class ends, I fly out the door, only to run into…

"I thought you were sick," my favorite brat says, putting her hand on her hip at an angle that makes it impossible not to notice her Gucci bracelet, complete with tag.

"It must have been a twenty-four hour thing," I say, trying to head to AP Geography.

"You know, you can't be at school if you've thrown up in the last day," she says.

"Well then, what are you and the rest of the cheerleaders doing here?" I ask innocently.

I brush past her before she can respond. Sierra is not great at comebacks, as they require actual thought.

The rest of the day is a blur. Spanish, Health and English become one continuous class despite being taught in two different languages, and I don't even remember lunch. All I can think about is *Scrambled Eggs*. I think I've come up with every worse-case scenario I can, one of which involves terrorist hackers and the FBI. That one's not even in the top five.

I drive straight home after the final bell, pulling into the garage and throwing open the door. I hit the stairs and go straight to my room, with Ringo hot on my heels. I toss my backpack in the corner and crawl onto my bed, staring up at the ceiling hoping to see inspiration. Unfortunately, all that's up there are about a hundred spitballs from when Carly Fife taught me how to make them in 4th grade.

Ringo jumps on the bed and curls up next to me. My three-a.m. bedtime is starting to catch up with me. I know I have Pre-Calc to do, and an English paper to start. Then again, after *Scrambled Eggs*, I'm wondering if I should ever write anything ever again.

I'm still staring up at my spitballs when there's a knock at the door. It's Lana, and I pull myself off my bed to let her in.

"Hey Morgan," she says. "Just FYI, we're eating dinner together again."

"No," I groan. I can't take any more Tannunbum Together Time. I know she's right though, because I can hear Dr. Phil coming from downstairs. He's using his, "I'm Confronting You About Your Actions" voice, which means Mom is glued to the TV.

"Heroin addict son or pregnant daughter?" I ask Lana, who is also listening.

"Both," she says. "And they're homeless."

We look at each other and sigh. Lana hates family meals as much as I do, although it's not because the food reminds her of excrement. She just hates eating in front of people. If Mom keeps this up, we'll be consuming crappy health food together for at least the next couple of days.

"What's she making?" I ask.

"I think she's trying Veggie Pizza again," said Lana.

"Pizza is not supposed to have veggies on it!"

"She said 5:45," she says, heading out the door. "See you then, sis."

Have I mentioned I hate my life?

The veggie pizza is everything I remember and worse. It's green. *Green.* How the hell is it pizza if there's no sauce and no cheese?

Things have gone downhill pretty quickly since Lana told me about our family meal tonight. It turns out that not only were the Dr. Phil guests homeless, they also had a mother with bipolar disorder and a tragic story involving the selling of a family heirloom to pay for medical bills.

At this rate, we'll be eating together for a month.

"Morgan, go get your father and tell him dinner is ready," Mom says, setting down four plates of this so-called pizza. Somewhere in Italy, a peasant is rolling in his grave.

I head upstairs and knock on the bathroom door. I don't actually know if he's there or not, but it's probably a good guess.

"Yeah?"

Men. So predictable.

"Mom's done with supper," I say.

"Be right down," he calls through the door.

Actually, I'd be more than ok with him just staying in the bathroom throughout the entire meal. I would rather hear Mom and Lana obsess over the grams of fat in their dinner than have to sweat through another discussion of *Scrambled Eggs*.

I sit down to face my punishment. It looks like a garden is growing on my plate. Damn you, Dr. Phil.

It's not looking like my wish for Dad to get a sudden case of the runs is going to work out for me, either. He's coming down the stairs with a giant stack of paper in his hands.

"I am in love with this script," Dad announces, plopping *Scrambled Eggs* down on the table. "This protagonist has such interesting family relationships…she feels like she doesn't belong, like her parents don't value her…it's teen-movie gold."

I can feel my heart pound faster and faster, and my deodorant is no match for the massive amounts of sweat beginning to form under my arms. I'm desperate to hide the fact that I'm terrified, and I'm sitting on my hands because I don't want anyone to see that they're shaking. At least I learned my lesson yesterday –I will be hanging on to every word that comes out of Dad's mouth.

"Who wrote it?" Lana asks from across the table, fingering through her copy.

I don't know how she knew to ask that, but I'm glad she did. I swear we have the same brain sometimes.

"I don't know," Dad says, and my heart rate drops significantly. "It's some pseudonym…Avery said it didn't sound familiar to him, either."

My shoulders drop in relief. I'm safe –for now. Unless he does know and he's just playing along to make me miserable, in which case I'm already screwed. And I still have all of dinner to fake through. My hands are still trembling, and I'm sweating like an old man in a sauna.

"Lana, I'd really like you to consider auditioning for Meagan," Dad says. "She's a wonderful role, really. She's this very complicated, multi-layered character. I find her so horrendously awkward, though…I think that'll sell with audiences."

Thanks, Dad. Love you, too.

"I don't think I'm what the author had in mind," Lana says, taking a bite out of the pizza.

"Why not?" Dad asks, setting his fork down. Uh-oh. Dad putting his utensils back on the table means he doesn't agree with you and is about to argue his point to the death. Unfortunately, Dad seems to think his point of view is the only point of view, and *you're* the illogical one for not seeing things the way he does.

"Well," Lana says, staring right back at him. She and my Mom are the only ones who can go to battle with Dad and come out in one piece. "I finished it, and I don't think I'm a good choice."

Wow. That was fast. That's kind of unusual for her, to have read a script this early. She was probably just looking for reasons to turn it down. I'm ok with that. She's not what I would want for Meagan. She's pretty. And skinny, even if she really doesn't think so. She doesn't bring that up with me, though. It's the one thing we don't talk about.

"Why aren't you a good choice?" Dad asks, silverware still firmly planted on the table.

"I'm not sure physically if I can pull it off," she says.

"The magic of make-up," he says. "Look at Charlize Theron. She was totally believable as Aileen Wuornos."

Great. Not only am I the ugly duckling, I'm a freaking serial killer. This just keeps getting better and better.

Lana tries another angle. Clearly she doesn't want this role. "She's supposed to be 16, right?"

"Yes," Dad says, cautiously.

"I don't think I can pull off sixteen," she says. "And the author's description of her doesn't sound like me."

"What do you mean, doesn't sound like you?"

"I don't think I match what the author had in mind," Lana says, clearly hinting at words she doesn't want to say aloud.

Dad has no such reservations and says, "Oh. You mean that she's fatter than you?"

I cringe twice. First off, fat is not a word that should ever be used around Lana. Ever. She's got enough issues. Second, I'm not exactly obese over here. I'm a perfectly healthy, totally normal size six. I'm not fat. I'm just not Lana. Why doesn't anybody get that? Besides, Dad is one to talk. He's not exactly hitting the gym every day, either.

"It's insignificant," he continues. "She can be whatever we want."

"I think it matters," Lana counters. "Besides, once you find the author, they'll get creative control and can veto anything you say, especially a major change to the script."

"The character's BMI is not a major change."

"It changes everything," Lana says, her voice rising. I don't know why she's so angry. It's probably because she actually ate most of the pizza and she's feeling guilty.

I'm the one who should be angry, and I am. Actually, I'm fuming. Aileen Wuornos, my ass. Like, what the hell? Thanks, Dad, I'm so glad you think I'm ugly. And awkward. And fat, at least compared to Lana and Mom. Just because it's all true doesn't mean it needs to be pointed out.

Lana, visibly upset, interrupts my mental rant and stands up from the table. "May I be excused?"

Mom, who has been silent, says yes and my sister gets up to leave, heading straight to the bathroom. Lana is getting rid of those horrible calories so they don't end up on her tiny butt. She'll be opening up the cupboard and downing a laxative or two, praying she won't end up with the horrible life of someone who can't count all of her ribs.

I ask to be excused as well, even though I've barely touched my pizza. I'm fighting the urge to flee, worrying if I just get up and run Mom and Dad will figure out *Scrambled Eggs* and I'll feel even crappier than I already. Thankfully Mom doesn't notice that the monstrosity she put on my plate hasn't gotten any smaller, and she permits me to leave. I run upstairs and head to my bookshelf, only to remember that in my panic last night I never replenished my junk food stash. A few handfuls of Cheese-its is not enough food after that stressful of a conversation. I grab my keys and head to the garage, careful not to pass the kitchen.

I go out to my car, stopping only to yell out to my parents that I'm going out and I'll be back. I make sure to slam the door as soon as I'm done shouting, just so they can't speak up and stop me.

Just in case they are bound and determined to keep me in the house, I start my car as quickly as possible and peel out of the driveway, heading down our street.

I don't bother to look back.

Chapter 4:

"There's nothing you can do that can't be done." –The Beatles, All You Need Is Love

I drive straight to a fast-food joint and get something real to eat: a burger, some fries and a banana smoothie. I had originally planned on eating my contraband in my room, but on the way out I realize that getting it all the way through the house and upstairs undetected would be next to impossible. I'm good, but I'm not that good. Besides, even if I did manage to sneak it inside, Ringo would tackle me and ruin my plans. The only thing Ringo likes more than processed cheese is a hamburger topped with processed cheese.

I'm out in the parking lot by now, and I actually stop and turn around, thinking I'll just head back inside and use one of the booths. There isn't much of a crowd, and it won't be tough to find an open seat. Usually, I'm the anti-Lana: I have no qualms about eating in front of people. I refuse to apologize for the fact that I actually consume food. But Dad's commentary tonight stung a lot more than the usual crap I get from Sierra and her pathetic wannabes. Maybe it's because I know he was telling the truth. Sierra and the other FTWAs (Future Trophy Wives of America) will say anything to get a reaction. They don't care if it's the truth, they care that it hurts. But Dad didn't know he was talking about me. He thought he was talking about Meagan Tatum, the awkward, sarcastic loser who doesn't buy her jeans in the children's section. If that's how my own father sees me, what the hell do I look like to everyone else?

I've lost all desire to head back into the restaurant, but my hunger is still running rampant. The food is warm in the bag, and I can feel the heat rising beneath my fingers. I climb into my car and turn on the overhead lights, illuminating the front seat. After turning on the radio, I set down the bag and begin downing the contents, the salt and oil of the French fries sending my tongue into its own little happy dance. Before I know it, every last crumb is gone. Making sure I've left no evidence of my secret meal in the front seat, I throw the wrappers away in the trash can outside the building.

I go back to my car and just sit there, wondering what to do next. The ten minute drive here, the fact that I actually have food in my stomach and Adele rocking out on the radio have all let me mellow a bit, and now I'm not so angry. I still just really, really don't want to go home.

Remembering my quest for junk food, I drive to a supermarket and pick up all the good stuff, especially the squeeze cheese I love. I'm not sure where I'll be able to hide the cylinder-shaped bottle, but I'm sure I can find somewhere out of Ringo's reach.

As I head toward the check-out, I pass by the pharmacy. One of the displays makes me pause. It's a huge selection of laxatives, including the bottle Lana keeps in our bathroom. Right next to this section are the vitamins, with everything from the cartoon character gummies for kids and the horse pills they make for nutrition junkies.

My brain sparks, and I veer off my path toward the counter and turn to the vitamin section. I know what Lana's laxatives look like –they're huge, grainy pills that look like they're made of a bunch of grass squished together. I don't know how she even gets them past her tongue.

Most of the vitamin bottles are clear, and I can see what's inside. After enough roaming, I find what I'm looking for. I turn over the bottle of BodyByNutrition Complete and read the label. It appears to have a large percentage of the daily values of vitamins A, B, and most of the rest of the alphabet. It also doesn't seem to have claims to induce weight loss. Perfect.

Just in case, I grab a bottle of Lana's laxatives and read the directions. It sounds like at most Lana would take two. Lana is a rule follower. She would never take more than the instructions told her. The vitamins also say to take two at the most. Awesome.

I take the bottle with me, throwing it in my basket among the cookies, crackers and, of course, Cheese-its. I head to the check out and pay using my debit card, the one Mom pays for every month without looking at the bill. Usually I just use it to buy books. I think this is more worthwhile.

Walking out into the parking lot, I get in my car and painstakingly arrange all of my junk food in my backpack, which I was smart enough to bring down with me from my room. Throwing out most of my thicker books, I put the crackers in between my Pre-

Calc and APGeo folders, my cookies by my Chem binder, and the squeeze-cheese ends up in my black water bottle. The vitamins I put in the front pocket.

With all this arranged, I drive home, pulling into the garage and walking in the front door with my backpack hoisted on my shoulders and my books in my arms. My parents are sitting in the living room watching a movie. I feel like such a spy, sneaking fattening food past the Hitler of nutrition.

I head upstairs, dropping off my backpack and taking out the vitamins. Making sure Lana is nowhere in the vicinity, I go into the bathroom and lock the door. I pull open the cupboard and pull down her laxatives. The bottle is almost full. Perfect.

I pour the pills out, trying to keep the sound to a minimum. I open the safety seal on the vitamins and see that my match was almost dead on. Hopefully she won't be able to tell the difference. I pour the entire bottle of vitamins into the laxative container, then scrape all of Lana's original pills I can carry into my hand and plop them into the toilet. Afraid I'll clog it, I put the other half of the pills in the sink, crushing them with my anti-acne facial wash bottle and running the water, watching my sister's demons float down the drain. Once those are gone, I flush the toilet and put the laxative bottle, now filled with what will probably be Lana's only consistent source of nutrients, away in its original position.

With that done, I return to my room and reluctantly begin my Math, half-heartedly calculating the radius of a circle inscribed in a polygon. It's almost midnight by now, and I'm losing my battle with the urge to sleep. My three-a.m. rendezvous with Lana is coming back to haunt me, and the whirring of my fan slowly carries me into unconsciousness.

I plop into my chair five minutes early for Pre-Calc the next day. No need to get another tardy. I am *not* up for janitorial duty after school.

As I pull out my math binder and book, my friend and Improv co-conspirator Shawn comes through the door, plopping his bag on the floor next to the seat in front of mine.

"Hey!" he says, seeing me. "I didn't get a chance to ask yesterday…what happened at Speech? Sierra came in and told us you were practically dying in Mrs. Kay's room!"

"Oh," I say. "Sorry about that! It was just a little flu bug, that's all. Must have been something I ate. Did you do ok without me?"

"Not so much," he says, grinning. "We drew "Spy Movie" for a topic and Seth ended up the Bond girl."

"Oh man," I laugh. Seth is 6'5, plays lineman and can bench press me. (Literally. We tried it once during a particularly unproductive practice. It worked great till I fell off and sprained my wrist.) "I can't imagine that went too smoothly."

"Actually, he ended up carrying Bond off into the sunset, which got a few laughs. Still, we could've used an actual girl. And by the way, Wix wants us to schedule a make-up practice."

Mrs. Wixton, or Wix, is the assistant speech coach and the improv "zookeeper". She signed on to help coach us after Mrs. Kay decided the improv teams couldn't handle practicing without supervision. (This may or may not have been shortly after the human bench press experiment.)

"Ok," I say. Actually, practice sounds nice. I can blow off some steam, get my mind off *Scrambled Eggs* for a while and have an excuse to not be at home. "Can we do after school today?"

"I think so," says Shawn. "I'll text and ask, but we should be ok. Want to just meet in Wix's room?"

"Sounds good," I say, just as the bell rings. Shoot. I've been too wrapped up in this conversation to finish the last of my math problems. For the second day in a row, I won't have a math assignment handed in. In my defense, it's six months into the school year and it's also the second assignment I've failed to do total, but still. Mr. Holland gives me a strange glance when I don't turn anything in to him.

He talks more about geometry today, and I try my hardest to pay attention and take good notes. It's better than yesterday, but I still find my mind wandering back to *Scrambled Eggs*.

As soon as the bell rings, I start to head out the door, but he stops me.

"Morgan?" he says.

I turn around slowly. Here it comes, the "I'm Concerned About You And Your Well-Being" speech.

"Yeah?"

"Morgan, is everything ok?"

I stare at him, hoping my silence will make this move faster.

He goes on. "You seem…distracted. You're not doing your assignments. You're not paying attention in class. You're not making your usual color commentary about my writing on the divider. What's up?"

He wrote on the divider and I missed it? I always give him crap for writing on the divider. Darn. Apparently my autopilot skills need some work.

"Everything's fine," I say. What am I supposed to do, explain it?

"Are you sure?"

"Yes," I say, trying to sound like I think he's crazy.

"Are you sure you don't want to talk with Mrs. Gold?"

Hell no. Mrs. Gold is about 10,000 years old. I'm pretty sure she dated Moses, and then Moses broke up with her because his mom didn't want him going out with an older woman.

"No," I say. Wait… "I mean, yes. I mean, I'm fine."

I'm not flustered over the thought of him finding out about *Scrambled Eggs*. Mr. Holland could stand here all day guessing and never come close. I'm flustered over the possibility of being forced to talk with a woman who routinely goes on rants about teenagers spending too much time on Spacebook and MyFace.

"OK," he says. "I'll give you a couple of days. But if things don't improve…" he says. "You're talking to Mrs. Gold, whether you like or not."

"Fine," I say. "Can I get an excused tardy to Geography AP?"

Mr. Holland obliges, and I leave pronto before he can change his mind. The bell has rung, and there are very few students left in the hallways. The announcements are already being read over the loudspeaker, and the monotone voice of our principal, Mr. Rooney, is crackling over the PA.

I find my seat in Mr. O'Malley's room just as Mr. Rooney finishes up his commentary on how well our wrestling team did at their meet last night. As soon as he signs off, R.J. Garrison shouts across the room with gleeful innuendo:

"Hey Morgan, did Mr. Holland help you out with your *Math*?"

The class makes one collective moan at my expense. Why do they think everything is a sex joke? I can't stand R.J. He's the dumb jock stereotype live in living color, although said color is a little pale this morning. He's probably hung over. Again. He's Sierra's boyfriend (shocker there, right?) and also just a jerk. He's that special kind of d-bag who'll pick on a special ed kid who's a third his size just because he can.

Luckily for me, Mr. O'Malley steps in and begins class before R.J. can throw any more insults at me. He kills the lights and turns on the projector overhead. AP Geo is usually really interesting, and today is no exception. We're talking about globalization and pop culture, and we're watching *The Lady and the Tramp* –in Chinese with English subtitles.

The Lady and the Tramp was one of Lana and my's favorite movies when we were little, and I still have most of the dialogue memorized. The Chinese, while sounding completely nonsensical to me, is coming out of actors whose voices are very similar to the originals, and the inflection is almost the same on most of the lines. This means I don't need to see the movie to actually understand what's going on, and I lay my head down on the desk.

I can already tell it's going to be a long day.

Chapter 5:

"It won't be long/til I belong/to you" –The Beatles, It Won't Be Long

"So how was your day?" Lana asks as I climb into the car.

"Crappy," I say, not feeling like giving any effort beyond that.

"How so?" she asks, maneuvering her way out of the FDR High parking lot.

Oh, where to start?

Probably with me falling asleep in the middle of Geography. I mean, in all fairness, how was Mr. O'Malley expecting us not to? It was dark, it was only second period, and we were watching a movie I've seen ten thousand times already. I almost got busted when he came over and asked what was happening in the movie, but my superb knowledge of Disney films saved my hide. By the time I started into how the story of the upper-crust Lady falling for the wrong-side-of-the-tracks Tramp was a metaphor for cooperation even during times of high tensions between social classes, he gave up and left me alone. Score one for the improv skills.

Things pretty much went downhill from there. Not only did R.J. decide to throw out more commentary through the rest of our shared classes, he seemed particularly intent on tossing it on me. Then the improv practice I'd been looking forward to had to be moved to Friday after school because of meetings going on in Wix's room. Combine that with a horrific semester test score in Spanish and a super-awkward Health first aid demo, and my day has essentially been a steaming pile of crap.

As I finish my rant, I realize Lana and I are not headed toward the house.

"Where are we going?" I ask.

"Dress shopping," Lana says. "Remember?"

Crap. Immersed in my own drama, I've completely forgotten that I've agreed to go to the winter formal with Sophie. She and her boyfriend of six months broke up last week, leaving poor Sophie with a brand new dress and no one to go with. I hate dances, and dresses for the most part, but I couldn't leave poor Sophie, so I sucked it up and am now on my way to do some shopping. Wahoo.

At least it's with Lana. Not only does she totally know what she's doing, she doesn't make me feel like crap about actually having curves. Mom and I stopped going shopping together a while ago. It was hell for the both of us. She with her size-six daughter (oh, no! She has boobs! Whatever shall we do?) and I with my mother awkwardly trying on dresses far too young for her and still looking hotter than me in them.

Lana pulls into an uptown boutique.

"Isn't this a little fancy for winter formal?" I ask.

"No," she says. "Now come on."

She practically drags me inside. As soon as we enter, a saleswoman recognizes Lana and runs over excitedly.

"Hello, Miss Tannunbum," she says, obviously not knowing Lana on a personal basis. Lana does not like to be called Miss Tannunbum. "How can I help you and your friend today?"

"We're sisters, actually," Lana says, smiling. "And I think we've got it covered. Thanks, though."

"Oh," the woman says. "You're sisters?"

"Yeah," I say. "We really are."

No one ever believes that. They usually say some stupid comment about being adopted or only sharing one parent or something.

This salesperson is, to her credit, wiser than this and settles simply for a quizzical look.

"Well," she says. "If you need anything, just let me know."

Lana begins searching the racks like a Navy SEAL, dragging me along as she searches for a dress to complete Mission Impossible: make Morgan look attractive.

After five minutes, she has a handful of dresses in her arms and leads me to the back of the store. They are all gorgeous –at least on the models in the pictures. On me – well, that could be a very different story.

Lana shoves me into a dressing room, handing me a blue dress with black embroidery.

"Start with this," she says.

I do, putting it on. After one glance in the mirror, it comes right back off. I look like a box. A really big box.

The next outfit up is bright pink (eww.) and purple (still eww.) It looks like it belongs in a four-year-old's dress-up box. Unfortunately, I also look like a four-year-old in it, with the shoulders and hips far too large on me. I look like a little girl trying on her mommy's clothes. (I, for the record, cannot wear my mommy's clothes. I outgrew the little girls' section years ago.)

I don't have much hope for the last dress, either. I throw it on just to satisfy Lana and step outside into the mirrors.

You know those stories where the girl thinks she's ugly and then she gets that perfect dress? When she steps out of the changing room and everyone in sight feels their jaw hit the floor?

Yeah, this isn't one of those stories.

I do look ok, though. The bright orange is, by some miracle, not clashing with my pasty skin, and Lana has picked out a cut that somehow flatters me. It's tight around the waist, and I'm pleasantly surprised to notice that I actually have one. A waist, I mean. I'm usually clad in a baggy T-shirt and jeans, and this is the first garment I've worn in a long time that's hugged my skin. My hair still looks like a bird's nest, but overall, I look far less awful than I was expecting.

Lana is excited.

"Morgan," she says. "You look hot!"

She's just being nice. But still, I can't help but stare at myself in the mirror.

I raise my arm to look at the tag poking into my side.

"Don't even think about it," Lana says. She's offered to foot the bill. I'm thinking this is why. I grumble over paying more than ten bucks for a t-shirt. We're in a pretty fancy boutique, one of the places that Lana herself goes with her friends when they have events to go to.

"Too late," I say, grabbing for the tag before she can stop me.

Actually, the number in front of me isn't too bad.

"Hey, this is pretty reasonable," I say, impressed. "Forty dollars seems ok."

"Morgan, sweetie," she says. "You're missing a zero."

I look back at the tag.

" $400? Who the hell pays $400 for a dress?"

Lana pushes me into back into the dressing room as I continue hollering. It's probably not the most appropriate response, but seriously? $400?

"First off," she says, after sushing me. "That's the list price designed to get people who can't afford it out of the store. Second, remember that charity gala I hosted a few months ago?"

"Which one?" I ask.

"Autism Speaks," she says. "With auctioning off some of my dresses?"

"Oh yeah," I say. "What about it?"

"That was here," she says. "And they got a load of free publicity from it, because a lot of the dresses I donated were from this boutique. They gave me a one-time 50% off deal because of it."

"Oh," I say. "But the dress is for me."

"Exactly," she says. "I like seeing you all dressed up. You can look pretty if you try, Morgan."

Now she's just being sappy.

"Now," she says. "Onto shoes."

"You don't think we've spent enough already?" I ask, incredulously.

"There is no point in wearing that gorgeous of a dress if you don't have some kick-ass shoes to go with it," she says, dragging me out into the main area of the boutique.

"Shouldn't I change first?" I ask. I'm not entirely comfortable walking around in a garment currently worth twice as much as my checking account.

"Oh, right," she says, temporarily letting me loose. "Go get into your normal clothes and meet me in the shoe section. Bring the dress."

"Why?"

"We need to see if it matches, silly!"

Oh. Right.

I gingerly remove the dress, careful not to let it touch the ground, get any of my sweat on it, or get breathed on. I arrange it on the hanger like a bomb squad technician, carefully planning every move. Once I'm assured that, barring an earthquake, the dress will not be going anywhere, I move much more quickly to toss on my own clothes. Zipping up my jeans and throwing on my Converse, I carefully take the dress and walk slowly out to where Lana is standing.

She has meticulously arranged a half a dozen pairs of shoes, mostly orange with varying decals, designs and levels of sparkles. She holds her hand out for the dress, and I give to her, careful not to let any part of it touch anything. She takes it and holds it over each box of bright-colored footwear, not saying a word as she slowly moves from pair to pair. After two or three minutes, she hands the dress back to me and takes three pairs away from the pile, including my favorites, the ones with the giant bow at the end.

"Why'd you get rid of those?" I ask.

"Oh, they're not even close to the right style," she says, with a wave of her hand. Lana understands fashion. Give me a quadratic equation and I'll kick its butt, but hand me Cosmo and I'm lost.

"So," she says, continuing to eye the dress, the shoes, and me. "Let's start with this pair. You're a size 10, right?"

She grabs two bright orange, very sparkly shoes. They look like what would happen if a bedazzler got stoned. But like I said earlier, I don't really know what I'm doing. I'm sure they are the highest of fashion.

I nod to Lana about my shoe size, and she looks to the shelves to find a pair that will work. I have giant feet, especially for only being five-foot-four and seventh-eighths of an inch. (So close to 5'5. So close!)

"Found some," Lana calls, standing on a stepstool. "Catch!"

She throws the box down to me, and I open it up to see that not only are they the Bedazzler-on-crack-shoes, but that the Bedazzler-on-crack shoes are high heels. Really, really high heels.

Lana must see the terror in my eyes, because she asks what's wrong.

I hold them up for her to see.

She stares back at me, not understanding my message.

I don't do heels.

Actually, that's not fair. I've never done heels. I've already sprained my ankle twice tripping over Ringo, and that was in Converse. I'm uncoordinated as is, and those sky-high heels are a recipe for disaster.

"Oh, come on," Lana says. "Try something new!"

Lana wears heels every day. She's wearing four-inchers right now, and she could probably do a perfect cartwheel. If I tried to do a cartwheel right now, most of the store would think I was having a seizure.

"Please," Lana says. "Do it for me."

She is paying for the dress, and I decide I owe it to her. I reluctantly slip off my sneakers and gingerly place one of the heels onto my foot. Gripping the shelf like a life preserver, I put my foot back on the ground and try to bring my other foot up to complete the set. By some miracle, I pull it off, and both my feet are on the ground in the vibrant orange shoes.

"I did it!" I practically shout. I never though I could pull off heels. This is actually really exciting…

"Not to kill the joy or anything," Lana says, cutting in. "But you'd better try walking first."

"Oh," I say. "Right."

Still holding onto the shelf, I pick up my left foot and put it down. So far so good. I do the same with my right. Granted, I look like a drunk giraffe, but still. Progress is progress.

"Ok," my sister says patiently. "Now let go."

Stupid enough to think I know what I'm doing, I step forward. With nothing to keep my balance, I throw my arms out to find nothing there. Watching me teeter forward, Lana lunges to try and support me, but her 90 pound frame is no match for my much heavier one, and we both end up in a heap on the floor.

"Oh my gosh!" The salesgirl from earlier is running over. "Are you guys ok?"

Lana and I are still trying to untangle ourselves. I'm trying not to stab her with my heels, and her spiked necklace is dangerously close to my wrist. Finally, our limbs separate and she rolls off of me.

We both say the exact same thing, as if on cue:

"Do you have them in flats?"

Chapter 6:

"Life is very short/and there's no time/for fussing and fighting my friends," – The Beatles, We Can Work It Out

The boutique does indeed carry the Bedazzler-on-crack shoes as flats, and Lana and I walk out of the store with a size 10 pair, the dress, and a necklace and earring set Lana insisted worked perfectly. I didn't quite understand what made it so different from the other three thousand silver necklaces hanging next to it, but whatever. She knows what she's doing. Lana wouldn't let me look at the receipt. She always buys me really nice Christmas and birthday presents, way more expensive than I can afford to buy her. She's the one who bought me Laverne, and Shirley, too.

We're in the SUV and on our way home, rocking out to the radio in blissful tune-deafness. Lana's voice cracks more than once, and so does mine, making for a gleefully awful rendition of Lady Gaga's latest hit.

When the station goes to commercial, Lana turns off the radio and turns to me as we speed down the freeway.

"So," she says. "After tonight we're free!"

"Thank God," I say. Mom and Dad are leaving for a three-day charity event in New York tomorrow night, leaving Lana and I with the house to ourselves.

"I don't think I could take any more of Dad trying to get me to take that role," she says, her eyes back on the road. "Like, seriously Dad, I'm not the girl you want."

My ears perk up. "Why not?" I ask, innocently.

"Because I don't think I'm anything like Meagan," Lana says.

"You weren't anything like that druggie, either," I say, mentally kicking myself as soon as the words leave my lips. What am I trying to do, convince her to take it?

Lana pauses, her perfectly manicured nails tapping the steering wheel as she struggles to explain. Finally, she answers with this:

"Meagan is very confident in who she is," Lana says, looking me straight in the eyes.

Lana being honest about her issues is an instance that's been getting rarer and rarer as we've grown up. Almost no topic is off limits during our midnight chats –we've talked about George Clooney's hotness, genocide in Sudan, and how George Clooney's hotness actually helps fight the genocide in Sudan. But we don't talk about the laxatives, the not eating, and the fact that our bathroom scale has been mysteriously smashed into pieces more than once. I know I should bring it up, try to stop it, since no one else in the Tannunbum house has bothered. My mother all but encourages it.

I guess that's not really fair. It's not all Mom's fault she turned out the way she did. For all my griping about my immediate family, we're a hell of a lot better than the homes my parents came from. Mom left her trailer-park family at fourteen when her alcoholic mother hit her one too many times, and met Dad when she was 21 and doing small modeling gigs. Dad was a struggling screenwriter also keeping his distance from a constantly-intoxicated parent, in this case his father. They met up, got married, had us, and found widespread success a few years later. Mom was the first and only woman Dad ever fell in love with. He's been with her for almost 25 years, and he's never spent time with any other woman, except for my grandma. And since Mom has always sucked at eating, and Lana has always sucked at eating, Dad pretty much assumes that girls just don't eat. (Seriously, Dad? Watch a Lifetime movie. *Any* Lifetime movie.) Basically, I'm the only person in the house who thinks Lana's got a problem...including Lana.

Maybe if I bring up her alter-ego she'll come clean. I give it a shot:

"Do you think you're anything like Laura?" I ask, returning her direct gaze.

Lana's eyes flash cold, not angry but almost unattached. The idea that she might be like the chronically dysfunctional Laura Tatum is creating a disconnect in her brain. The idea that maybe, just maybe she has a problem simply doesn't seem to be within the realm of possibilities.

"No," she says. "I don't really see the resemblance."

With that, she turns up the radio full blast and the rest of the ride goes by with only an autotuned Katy Perry to fill the silence.

The last Tannunbum family dinner for the next foreseeable future is certainly interesting.

Dad comes upstairs with an announcement.

"I've spent all day working through that script," he says. "I've decided to go for it."

Crap. Until now I had hoped that Dad would decide *Scrambled Eggs* was terrible and that he would give up on making it a movie. Apparently not. I feel like he would be making a much bigger scene if he knew I was the one who wrote it, but still. I'm sweating up a storm again, and I'm struggling to hold in my instinct to flee.

"Did you get the author's permission?" Lana asks.

"No," he says, and I sigh in relief. "We can't find them."

"Who does that?" Mom asks, taking a bite of tofu. "Write such a good screenplay and send it in without leaving their name?"

"Maybe they don't want their name attached," I say. Hint, hint.

"But then why would they send it in?" Mom asks.

Beats me. I'm not the one who did the sending.

Mom turns to Dad. "Has Avery tried tracing the postmark?"

"Yeah," Dad says. "No luck."

" It was sent by email from an untraceable account from an internet café," Lana adds.

Dad turns to Lana. "How did you know that?"

"You told me earlier, remember?" she says, brushing him aside. "Whoever sent it obviously didn't want their name attached."

Dang. Whoever sent in my screenplay was careful. When I find them, I'll have to thank them. (After I punch them.)

"So how are you going to make the movie?" Mom asks.

"Well, Avery's going to recheck every clue we've got," Dad says. "He's got to be out there somewhere."

"He?" I ask. "How do you know it's a he?"

"It's just the way it's written," Dad says. "It seems like the voice of a guy."

Awesome. So, so awesome.

"I don't think so," Lana says, her tofu still untouched. "This was totally written by a girl, and probably a younger one, too. Maybe even a teenager."

My heart about stops. This is bad. This is very, very, very bad. What is Lana doing?

"Isn't it told from the point of view of the girl, though?" I say, trying to keep my voice from shaking. "Like, isn't it supposed to sound like a teenager, no matter who wrote it?"

"Yeah," Dad says, pleased to see I agree with him. I just want his mind far away from the idea that *Scrambled Eggs* was written by an actual hormonal, puberty-stricken kid and not an adult pretending to be one.

"No matter what the gender or age of the author," Mom interjects. "You have to find them if you want to make this movie."

"Oh, we're making the movie," Dad says. "We've got to snap it up before somebody else does. Avery has checked with some other agents, and for some reason he's the only one who's got a copy."

"That he's been told," Mom interrupts. "If it's really as good as you say it is…"

"It is," both Lana and Dad say.

"…Then other production companies may be sitting on it in hopes of beating you to the author." Mom finishes.

I haven't thought about this possibility. Could other people be looking for me, too? I'm not quite as worried about this scenario, as most of those people don't happen to live with me. If my own father can't recognize my life in a screenplay, I'm probably ok.

"Well, then," Dad says. "Avery and I will just need to work faster. We've got an all-out manhunt planned to find this guy."

"Girl," Lana interjects. "This was a girl. Period. No guy could write an authentic female character like Morgan, sorry," she catches her mistake. "Meagan."

That was not an innocent slip-up. She knows. And she's about to give me away!

Chapter 7:

"I want to be a paperback writer" – The Beatles, Paperback Writer

Thankfully, Dad doesn't seem to notice her name mix-up, or the fact that I am very nearly hyperventilating.

"Fine," he says. "Person. We've got an all-out manhunt planned to find this person."

"What do you mean, all-out manhunt?" I ask, my pulse somehow getting even faster.

"An analyst and a private detective, probably," he says. "We need to find this author soon."

I ask to be excused, and I leap from the table as soon as Mom says it's ok. I hear Lana ask to do the same as I run up the stairs, and I turn around and stop her as soon as she's out of my parents' sight.

Dragging her into my room, I say to her, "What was that about?"

"What?" Lana looks confused. "What are talking about? Let go of me!"

I oblige, but I don't lower my voice.

"I know you know," I say. "About *Scrambled Eggs*. You practically told them!"

"Oh," Lana says. "That."

"Yeah," I say, struggling to keep my voice down so my parents won't hear. "*That*. Did you tell Dad?"

"No," she says.

"How did you know?" I ask.

"What is this, the Spanish inquisition?" Lana asks, defensively.

"You *know*. 'Morgan, sorry, Meagan'? Lana, you know I'm behind that script, you basically gave me away! How did you know I wrote *Scrambled Eggs*?"

"It was a hunch," she says, averting my glare.

"A hunch?" I ask, incredulously. "Lana, that's not good enough. I need to know! How did you figure it out?"

She is silent.

Suddenly, I put the pieces together: How she knew it was a teenage author. How she knew how it was sent, even though Dad didn't know she knew. Why she got the names mixed up.

"Holy hell," I say, realization hitting me in the face. "You knew because you sent it to him!"

Lana gives a miniscule nod.

"You did this. You did this to me! Lana, why? Why the hell would you steal my work, and then send it to my own freaking father? What is wrong with you?"

How could she do this to me? Betray me like this, send my life tumbling upside down…for what? It's not like she's got anything to be jealous of. She's Lana Tannunbum –the epitome of young grace and class, a rising Hollywood star. You know what I'm the epitome of? The reason health insurance policies should not cap costs for ER visits.

"Give me an answer, Lana," I say, voice filled with disgust. "Why would you do this?"

"Because you're too damn good to be ignored anymore," she says, turning to me.

"Oh," I say, in a mocking tone. "So your plan was to totally ruin me by sending a script about how freaking awful my family is TO MY FAMILY? That's not the kind of attention I was really looking for!"

"Oh, Morgan," Lana says, her voice dropping. "It wasn't supposed to go to Dad."

"Then who was it supposed to go to?" I ask, voice rising higher. I have to be careful; Mom and Dad are still within earshot. Resorting to a forced whisper, I go on, "You sent it to Avery. It's a teen movie. Who else was it going to go to?"

"I was hoping someone else," Lana says, quietly.

"Oh, *hoping*," I say, sarcastically. "What a bummer it ended up with dear old Dad. You had no right to take this! This is my work! How did you even know it existed? I wrote on Laverne and it stayed there!"

"No, it didn't," Lana says, her voice now starting to match mine. "You had a hard copy."

What the hell? How does she know all this?

"Have you been spying on me?"

42

"No," she says. "You left it in my car on one of our Food Shelf nights. You had speech and were in a rush, and you ran out of my car so you wouldn't be late for musical theater. You left a manila envelope sitting in the back seat. I yelled after you but you were already gone. I opened it up to see if it was your music or something you would need."

"Ok," I say. "But then it wasn't. So you should've put it back and minded your own damn business."

Lana gives me a wary look.

"I know," she says. "But I started to read it and I couldn't stop. At first I thought it was one of Dad's, but really soon it was super obvious that the only person who could have written it was you. And I was hooked, Morgan. Absolutely hooked. I almost killed my car battery because I sat there in the parking lot right where I dropped you off for twenty minutes before someone honked at me to move. I pulled into a spot and read the whole thing that night while you were at speech. I couldn't just let something that good go to waste."

"Go to waste," I repeat, with an angry laugh. "Who gave you the authority to decide that? *Scrambled Eggs* was supposed to stay on Laverne. I would never choose to let the whole world read it."

"Well, I would never choose to have someone take my life, pick out all my worst qualities and splash them all over the page. Ever think about that?" Lana fires back. "Whether or not you wanted it to be read, what you wrote has consequences."

Stung, I shoot back.

"Yeah, well so does treating me like the fourth wheel in this family for so long!"

Lana now has tears in her eyes.

"So you don't feel the least bit guilty about what you wrote?"

I do, actually, but I'm too pissed to admit it. Instead, I fire back:

"You don't feel this least bit guilty about stealing my work?"

She is quiet.

"I hope you're happy, Lana. I really hope you are. Just in case you needed any more proof that you're the best and most-loved kid in this house by a long shot, here's a crapload of evidence. Just in case you weren't absolutely sure of your superiority over me, here you go. You. Are. Better. Message received. Now get the hell out."

"Of your room?" she asks, stomping off. "No problem."

"Of my life," I say. "And if you tell Dad about *Scrambled Eggs*, I'll tell him about the bathroom scale."

With that, I slam the door behind her.

Suddenly, all of my remaining anger (and there's plenty of it) melts, and I'm left with an overwhelming urge to cry. Tears spring up into my eyes, and before I know it I'm sitting on the floor of my room sobbing uncontrollably.

Damn it. I am *such* a teenager. What the hell is wrong with me? I'm a big girl; I can handle crap on my own. So why am I sitting here like crying will help me get anything done?

Here's the thing. I can count the number of times I've cried on my fingers. The last time was almost two years ago, when Grandma Tannunbum died. I made it through *My Sister's Keeper* (the book), *A Walk to Remember* (the movie) and *Where the Red Fern Grows* (both) without tearing up. I do have a soul. I really do. I just don't get upset easily, I guess.

But tonight is different. I think I'd actually rather be Mandy Moore's character than me right now. At least then I'd have a super hot guy in love with me.

I am hopelessly, totally toast. Every scenario here does not end well for me. I'm like a caged bear, stuck without any escape routes. If Lana doesn't go right downstairs and tell Dad I wrote *Scrambled Eggs*, he'll figure it out if he reads it enough times or hires those private investigators. Any of those end in him and Mom and Lana hating me forever.

Actually, I may have already achieved that last one. I do feel bad about how I portrayed my family in *Scrambled Eggs*. I wrote it when I was angry, and it's definitely not the kindest script ever written. But that did not give her the right to just go and take it from me. And I still don't know how she got it. Whatever. I don't even care if she's mad at me. As far as I'm concerned, she's persona non grata in here. But as angry as I am at her, the idea that I now truly have no one in this house makes me cry even harder.

As I grab another tissue, I make sure that my sobs are quiet. No one can know I'm up here bawling my eyes out.

I guess that's how we Tannunbums deal with problems: silence.

Chapter Eight:

"Hey Jude/don't make it bad/take a sad song/and make it better" – The Beatles, *Hey Jude*

A few minutes into my monsoon of tears, I realize I've forgotten my lifeline, the person who always helped me deal with this crap. I pick up my cell phone and call Katie, struggling to see her name on the contact list through my tears.

She picks up on the second ring.

"What's up girl?"

I try to speak, I really do. But I can't, and all poor Katie hears are my sobs.

"Oh, honey," she says, immediately switching into emotional emergency mode. "What's wrong?"

I think I can speak at this point, but I realize I don't know what to say. How the hell am I supposed to describe this?

Katie's voice, full of worry, fills the phone.

"Um…nobody died or anything…right?"

I get why she's concerned. The last time I called crying my eyes out was when Grandma Tannunbum passed away.

"No," I say.

"So Lana's fine?"

"Yeah." Maybe not after I get through with her, but for now.

"And Ringo?"

"Yeah."

"And your Mom and Dad?"

"Yeah."

"Alright," she says, assured that there has not been a major catastrophe. Filling in the blanks as she always does, she blurts out, "Did the shit hit the fan?"

"Yeah," I say, a little bit of a giggle escaping my lips.

"Were you the fan?"

"Yeah," I say, almost smiling now. I love Katie.

"Ok," she says. "Breathe, girl."

"She stole my…diary!" I burst out. A journal seems like the closest analogy I can draw to *Scrambled Eggs*.

"Who's she?" Katie asks.

"Lana!" I say, a rush of air leaving my lungs. "I can't believe she would do this to me. She had no reason to, I don't understand…"

Words tumble out of my mouth like rocks, although I manage to avoid mentioning *Scrambled Eggs*. I sound like the drunk relative present in every family, the one who gets weepy after a few too many bourbons during the annual Christmas dinner. Even I want to slap me.

Luckily for me, Katie is in Chicago and can't smack me across the face. I don't think she would even if she were here, and just knowing she's on the other end of the line is comforting. Eventually, I just start sobbing, and Katie listens patiently as I work through my crap.

Finally, I regain my composure, and my friend starts to gently pry.

"Do you know why she took it?" she asks.

"No," I say.

"Is there anything in there you didn't want her to read?" she asks.

"Um…pretty much the whole thing," I confess. "The entire…*diary* is me in rant mode."

"Ooh," Katie says. I can practically hear her cringing. "So I'm guessing it wasn't the kindest."

"Let's go with no," I say.

"Oh boy," Katie groans. "So you're really pissed she stole it –which you totally have the right to be –and she's really pissed about what you wrote."

"Pretty much," I say.

"Sucks to be you, huh?"

(Katie doesn't mince words.)

"Yeah," I say, with a little giggle.

"I'm sorry," she says. "Want me to come beat her up for you?"

"Yes!" I say. "And then stay here. Forever."

"I wish," she says, with a groan. "I have a 120 point essay test in Western Civ in two days. Paragraph after paragraph of regurgitated information on Alexander the Great. I can't even deal."

"120 points? That's just mean," I say, trying to commiserate.

"Yeah," she says, with a laugh. "Well, at least I'll get to write about his alcohol-fueled rages. That could be fun. Do you have any big tests coming up?"

And so we talk the rest of the night. We chat about everything under the sun: our classes, guys, and life in general while I guzzle a few sodas courtesy of the large-print edition of *War and Peace*. Katie is complaining about the snow and freezing temperatures, while I offer up a few grumblings about the questionable IQs of some of my school's honor students. Before we know it, it's 10:30 and Katie's mom is yelling at her to go to bed, because it's past midnight in Chicago.

"Ok," Katie says with a yawn. "So do you feel better?"

"Yeah," I say with a smile. "I do."

"Good," she says, with another yawn. "Now go to bed!"

She hangs up on me in her usual brash style.

Feeling good for the first time all day, I throw myself onto my bed and fall asleep with a smile, Ringo curled up beside.

I wake up with a start.

Good Lord, do I need to pee.

The three cans of Diet Mountain Dew two hours before bed was probably not a great idea in hindsight, and my bladder feels like it's about to explode. I jump out of bed and run into my bathroom, headed full speed for the bowl.

Damn it. There's no toilet paper!

Cursing myself for never replacing the roll, I run out of my room and run toward the family bathroom, throwing the door open and barely making it in time.

With my bladder no longer outweighing a bowling ball, I breathe a sigh of relief. The clock on the bathroom wall reads 3:30 am, and I'm about to crawl back into bed when I hear a sound coming from downstairs. It sounds like the heater, a constant swooshing noise but quieter and faster. I am not about to wake up with the heat dead, and I start heading downstairs to make sure that all is functioning correctly.

As I creep towards the stairs, I realize that the basement lights are on. That's really odd. Dad is an electricity Nazi. Despite the fact he made twenty million dollars last year, he makes us pay him five bucks for every light we leave on overnight.

I'm starting to get worried. Both Lana and Mom have some crazy fans, but not break-into-the-house crazy. At least, I don't *think* they're that crazy…

I'm starting to wonder if I should wake up Dad, but that's probably not a great idea. If (and more like when) I'm wrong, I will never be allowed to live it down. Still, I'm not going down there alone. I take a glance around for anything useful. Unfortunately I'm in the laundry room and all I've got is a plunger, a box of Tide and a bunch of Mom's Victoria's Secret push-up bras. (There's so much padding in there…how do her boobs even fit?) I settle on the plunger. It's not the greatest weapon ever, but it beats out Mom's gravity-defying underwear.

Now brandishing the pretty disgusting plunger, I silently open the door to the stairs and gingerly start down, standing on tip toes to avoid any creaking by our almost one-hundred-year-old house. The whirring noise is still humming along, although it's a little louder now that I'm closer. It's also accompanied by another sound –heavy breathing.

I jump back and press myself against the wall. There's definitely somebody down there.

It takes every ounce of control I have in my body to not run up the stairs and flee. I reach for my phone to call 911, but it's not in my waistband. Crap. Looks like I'm on my own. Inch by inch, I move toward the banister, praying the house won't squeak and give me away. Eventually, I'm in a prime position to see who's broken into my house and go ape on them with my plunger. I mentally prepare myself to kick this guy's behind with my improvised weapon. I pick it up and am ready to strike.

I am woman, hear me roar.

I peek up and about drop the plunger.

It's Lana running on the treadmill, her tiny legs wobbling under so much pressure. I drop to a sitting position in relief. It's a good thing I already heeded the call of nature, or I may have peed right there on the stairs. What is she doing? It's not like she actually ate anything to burn off.

Of course, that is my sister's M.O. Eat nothing, run, repeat. I'm really getting sick of it.

As I think that, though, I feel a twinge of guilt. I'm probably the reason she's down here. She's punishing herself.

Good, I think, before another sisterly pang of remorse hits. I basically told her she was a terrible person, and I'm pretty sure she already thinks she is. I did her no favors by yelling at her.

But she deserved it, I tell myself. When she took *Scrambled Eggs*, she knew there was a chance I'd discover what she'd done, and if I did I would be really unhappy with her. Well, she got caught and now she'll have to suffer the consequences. However she deals with those is on her, not me.

But even I don't buy that. Sure, I'm still plenty angry at her. But as I creep back up the stairs and go back to bed, it's the treadmill, not Lana, I want to tear apart.

Chapter Nine:

"I get by with a little help from my friends," –The Beatles, A Little Help From My Friends

By the time I get to school the next day, my focus has shifted from Lana's late-night treadmill session to the new AP Geo essay Mr. O'Malley has assigned us. The topic is "How the World Economy Affects Me". I *totally* want to write about my life right now. That hasn't come back to bite me at all.

I'm heading off to Spanish when Sierra stops me. Why won't she leave me alone? Doesn't she have make-up to refresh or a random guy's throat to stick her tongue down?

"Oh my gosh," she says, in a less judgmental tone than usual. "Is it just me, or did you drive off with Lana Tannunbum yesterday?"

What I want to say is, "No, that was the pot you were smoking."

What I do say is a simple "No."

I don't want anything to do with Lana at the moment. And even when I'm not fighting the urge to scream at her, I don't tell people we're related. Having a famous sister attracts people like Sierra, who want nothing to do with me and everything to do with Lana. It's way simpler for me to find out if people really like me or just my name if I keep Lana out of it.

"Wait," she says, pulling on my backpack as I try to walk away.

I turn around and glare at her.

"Oh my God," she says, her perfectly manicured hand reaching up to cover her mouth. "It was!"

"How did I not put that together?" she asks in a sticky-sweet voice. "You have the same last name! Are you like, second cousins or something?"

You know what, screw it.

"We're sisters."

"Oh my God," she says. "I didn't know you were adopted!"

Wow. Really?

Actually, it would make more sense if I was not a biological Tannunbum. There's Mom and Lana –two beauties who can get anything they want with the bat of an eye. Dad is brilliant with words and cinematography. My main skills are hiding junk food and getting cropped out of family photos in People magazine.

Sierra is following me now as I sprint up to Spanish. If she makes me late…

"So," she says, running behind me, the metallic beads on her oversized Prada bag jingling as we trot up the stairs. "What's she like?"

"Lana?" I ask, about to slide into Senora Sandara's class. "Oh, she likes walking the dog, and watching documentaries, and helping fundraise for charities."

I don't add "and totally wrecking her sister's life", even though I really want to.

"Oh," I add. "And you know what she really hates? Plastic, fake teenage girls."

With Sierra's face turning bright red, I return the dazzling smile she was shooting me minutes earlier and shut the door.

My after-school and evening hours are completely packed, and it starts with Improv practice. I welcome the relief, and I think Seth, Shawn and Alan do too. It's a Friday, and we can all tell: our senses of humor seem to be warped to the point that *anything* is funny. After about 45 minutes of continuous snickering on our part, Wix gives up and tells us to go home, but she's grinning too.

My next task is the one I'm least looking forward to: I have to run home to take a quick shower and grab my dress before heading to Sophie's. That girl is a wizard with hair and make-up, so I may actually end up looking ok. It was really nice of her to offer to help me, and I jumped at the chance to be anywhere but in my house.

I drive home and head inside, praying Lana is running errands or otherwise occupied. I don't want to have to see her, let alone talk to her.

Unfortunately, I spot her as soon I walk in. She's sitting on the coach watching a documentary on American poverty. However, she's pretty engrossed in the movie and doesn't seem to see me as I run up the stairs.

I go into my room, say hello to Ringo and head into my bathroom. Stepping into the shower, I give a valiant attempt toward shaving, suppressing the urge to yelp when I cut myself a few times. After narrowly avoiding a shampoo-in-eyes fiasco, I nearly slip and fall on my way out of the shower. I'm going to need Life Alert before I hit twenty.

Bleeding and looking as though I've just survived the Alamo, I grab a few Band-aids from my freshly stocked supply and throw on sweatpants and a T-shirt. Heading out into my room, I throw my shoes, tights and the accompanying jewelry Lana bought into a tote bag and strategically take my dress out of the closet. Grabbing my keys, I head out towards my car at an odd pace, trying to go fast enough to avoid having to talk to Lana but slow enough that my dress does not move an inch on the hanger.

Lana is still engrossed in her movie, but I think she sees me leave. She's probably ignoring me just as much I'm ignoring her. That's fine by me. As I get to the door, I yell back to remind her I'm going to Sophie's and then Winter Formal, and I could be pretty late. She doesn't answer, and I don't wait for a reply. I go to my car, carefully lay the dress in the backseat, throw my tote and purse in shotgun and drive over to Sophie's.

"Hey," she says, as I step inside. "That's a great dress!"

I grin. "Yeah, I really like it," I admit. Sure, it cost more than Laverne, but I do look pretty nice in it.

"Wait till we get the rest of you all dolled up to match," she says with a grin. "Come on!"

Grabbing my wrist, she drags me upstairs and into her room. The first thing she does is blow dry my hair, not a quick task thanks to its immense thickness and length. After that, she bars me from looking in a mirror so that I can "truly appreciate my own transformation". Over the next two hours, Sophie uses more creams, lotions, and powders than I knew existed at the Macy's make-up counter. She wrestles my stick-straight hair into an impressively complicated curly updo and paints my nails a sparkly silver. When she tries to put in the dangle earrings Lana bought me, we realize the holes have partially closed in the back. Not to be outdone, Sophie takes the earrings and jams them into my earlobes. Without ice. Or any warning, really. She just puts her whole weight into that one very small piece of metal and it eventually goes through. Painfully.

"Ok," she says. "That'll work."

She turns the stool around so I can finally see what she's done. I don't actually look that bad. I mean, relatively. The 20-odd products she appears to have put in my hair actually worked, and it's smooth under all that hairspray. My freckles are well-hidden and my skin is not its usual pasty shade. I still don't look like a Tannunbum, but at least I'm headed in the right direction.

"Oh my gosh," I say. "Thanks! You're the best."

"I know," Sophie says with a grin.

Thanking her once again, I run out of her room and change into my twice-the-value-of-everything-I-own dress while Sophie, who had already done a lot of her own hair and make-up, puts on the finishing touches and her dress. I slip on the sparkly flats after my tights and spandex, and presto –I'm ready.

Heading back to Sophie's room, I knock on the door and she lets me in. The sight of her dress nearly takes my breath away. It's a strapless purple number, and it hugs her voluptuous curves in an incredibly flattering way.

"Damn girl!" I say. "You got it going on!"

She grins. "I was just happy to find a dress for a girl with a D-cup that didn't show off A, B and C."

I laugh. Sophie is the most confident girl I've ever met –in a good way. She knows who she is and she owns it. I'm pretty jealous.

"Now," she says, grabbing her digital camera. "Time for pictures!"

"No…" I groan.

"Come on," Sophie says. "You know our moms will kill us if we don't."

"Yeah…" I say, reluctantly. "You're right."

"Yes, I am," she says. "Now pose like you're happy, darn it!"

I muster a smile, and Sophie snaps away, probably taking a hundred different shots. There might be one usable picture in the whole set. Bigfoot is more photogenic than I am.

Finally, Sophie is satisfied, and as she sets down the camera she looks at the clock.

"Hey, we better head out," she says. "You ready to go?"

"Yep," I say. "Let's roll."

I do have fun.

Sophie and I meet Rebekkah and Emilee at Greg's, an old-style family restaurant home to the world's most fantastic pizza. Rebekkah and Emily look fantastic – Rebekkah's short, willowy figure complemented by a one-shoulder aqua-blue dress and Emilee's taller, more filled-out body looking great in a red sparkly evening gown. We're decked to the nines and having a blast, actively engaged in a compliment war over who looks the best.

We all split a large and dig in, the homemade crust flaky and delicious. That's the other thing I love about my friends. Throughout the entire dinner, the words "calorie", "fat" and "unhealthy" go unspoken, and our conversation is mostly about guys, the latest rumors floating around school and how Mr. Klien's teaching style could be sold as a sedative.

Once we get to the dance, we rock out, kicking off our shoes and jumping to the music. We stay toward the back of the cafeteria, where the music won't render us deaf and away from the grinding couples. Eventually, my mind stops thinking about *Scrambled Eggs* and Lana and the treadmill and my whole messed up life and I just dance, losing most of my inhibition while doing the Cupid Shuffle.

Before I know it, it's past midnight and the dance is over. Throwing on my coat, I say goodbye to my friends and drive home, pulling into the garage when the clock says 12:10 am.

I open the garage door and step inside, shouting to Lana that I'm home. Usually I'd just sneak inside and shut the door, but since Mom and Dad are in New York, it's just the two quarrelling sisters for the night.

To my relief, I don't see Lana when I walk in. She's probably still ignoring me. Right back at you, sister. Ringo comes running down the stairs. I lean down to pet my pug and say, "Hey, buddy. Are you ready for bed?"

Ringo and I start to head up to my room. As I pass by the couch I see Lana's not there either, and it occurs to me I should probably make sure she's not on the treadmill. I pause; there's no noise downstairs. Good. That's the extent of my caring for tonight.

I make it up to my room and start to head inside when Ringo makes a sudden dash into Lana's room.

"Ringo," I groan. "Come on boy, time for bed."

Ringo doesn't come out of Pink Paradise but instead starts to bark, and loudly. He usually only does that when he needs to pee. Or he sees cheese.

"Ringo," I say. "Get out of there." (Even though I'm kind of wishing he'd do his duty on some of Lana's clothes just to piss her off, no pun intended.)

Ringo still doesn't come and only barks louder.

"Come on, Ringo…" I say as I start to open Lana's door.

What I see stops me cold.

Lana is lying motionless on her floor, a glass in her hand shattered.

Chapter 10:

"How does it feel to be one of the beautiful people?" –The Beatles, Baby, You're a Rich Man

I fling open the door and run inside. Lana's skin is even paler than it was earlier, and her lips are dry. Carefully avoiding the glass shards, I kneel beside her.

"Lana," I shake her delicate shoulders. "Lana, Lana, Lana."

"Go away," she mumbles, closing her eyes and rolling over, barely missing some large chunks of glass.

"Lana," I'm yelling now. "Open your eyes, open your eyes, open your eyes."

I stand there idiotically repeating the phrase until she finally does what I ask.

"What happened?" I ask, alarmed at how out of it she seems. The glass. Was she downing pills? "Lana, what did you do? What did you take?"

"Nothing," she says, in a barely audible whisper.

Her eyes flicker shut again. I shout at her to stay awake.

"Lana," I say. "Come on, we're going to the hospital, ok?"

"No," she says, like a four-year-old trying to avoid her way out of eating her vegetables.

I lean down on the bed and grab her shoulders, hauling her to her feet. I'm twice her size, and she's in no shape to resist me. As I get her into a standing position, her head lolls.

"Dizzy," she mumbles.

"I know, sweetie," I say. "I've got you, I've got you, I've got you."

I repeat it all the way to the garage, although I think I'm saying more to reassure myself. About halfway down the stairs, I realize I can just carry her, and I scoop my big sis into my arms. She's light as a feather, and her skin is almost see-through. I grab the keys to the SUV and put Lana in shotgun, making sure to buckle her in. I throw myself in the driver's seat and speed off, headed for the nearest ER, which is ten minutes from my house. (I know the route by heart by this point. Yours truly has tripped, fallen, and slammed-finger-ed her way into the Poor Coordination Hall of Fame.)

By some miracle, I don't get arrested for speeding, and I pull into the hospital and drive right up to the ER, opening the passenger side door and scooping Lana out again. My arms are starting to ache from carrying this paper doll of a girl, but the surge of adrenaline allows me to take the last few steps toward the entrance.

As soon as I step in the doors, people come seemingly out of nowhere and take my sister from my arms, placing her on gurney and whisking her away. I try to run after them but a nurse stops me, holding me back as my sister disappears around a corner.

"No!" I shout. "I need to go with her!"

The nurse, who can't be much bigger than me but is clearly much stronger, grabs my shoulders and says, "Calm down. I need to know what happened."

"ShewasjustlyingthereIdon'treallyknowwhathappenedshewastalkingfunnyand…"

She stops me.

"Slow down," she says. "Breathe."

I take a few deep gulps of air and repeat what I've just said, but slower. I don't mention that I think she might've tried to kill herself. I've gotta be wrong. She can't have…right?

"She was just lying there, and she was talking really weird and she was barely awake."

"Were you two partying together?" she asks, glancing down at my dress.

"For crying out loud, she's wearing Minnie Mouse pajamas!" I say, before I can stop myself.

"No," I add, a little sheepishly.

"Ok," she says. "It's Lana Tannunbum, right?"

"Yeah," I say. My sister is still recognizable, even if she seems to be auditioning to play Casper's body double.

"And you're her friend?" she asks.

"Sister," I say. Her horribly shitty, worst person in the history of the world sister.

She shoots me a look. "Nice try," she says, clearly not amused.

This is so not the time for this!

"No, we really are!" I say, eyes filling with tears. Not like I really deserve the title of "sibling" right now, but still. I reach down to take my driver's license out of my purse only to realize I've left both items in the SUV, which is still running outside.

Another nurse runs toward us. As she gets closer, I can see through my tear-blurred eyes that it's Mandy, one of the RNs I've run into more than once in my various clumsiness-fueled trips here.

"Oh boy," she says, grabbing my arm and leading me to a chair. I'm too busy balling to fight her. Turning to the other nurse, she asks, "What happened?"

"She brought in a girl she's claiming is her sister," the nurse says, still clearly attached to the idea that someone like me could not be related to someone like Lana.

Mandy is now kneeling beside me, her fingers on my wrist. "She's crying!" she implores, looking at me with concerned eyes.

"So?" the other nurse asks.

"She didn't cry when she broke her clavicle in two places trying to get out of a pencil skirt!"

Yeah. See my aversion to dresses now?

"Lana," I finally manage to say. "It's Lana. She's really, really...she's really, really sick and I don't know what's wrong and..."

I collapse into sobs again. Twice in three days. I'm not doing well on the whole not-crying front.

The other nurse turns to Mandy.

"Wait," she says. "They're really sisters?"

"Yes," Mandy says, wrapping her arms around me. "Come with me, sweetie."

The hour in the private waiting room is the longest sixty minutes of my life.

Mandy stays with me for as long as she can, but soon she has a patient to take care of, and she leaves me all alone. I stare at the beige walls, crying and praying and crying some more. What have I done? I *knew* Lana was self-destructing, I *knew* that she was struggling and I screamed at her about how horrible she was, unloaded all my anger in one shouting match. And then I saw her in the basement and I still didn't do anything, like I've never done anything to stop Lana from hurting herself. I just stand by and let it happen because I'm too damn scared I'll make her angry and lose the one good relationship I have and now…now I don't even know what's happening, but it's *my fault*. I did this. Whether or not it was a suicide attempt, I'm the one to blame. I either pushed her over the edge or failed to pull her back from it.

I am the worst human being ever.

Mom and Dad still don't know. I left messages for them, but neither one has called me back. They're probably in the middle of the event and won't check their phones for another couple of hours. My mind is racked with questions. I didn't see any pills near Lana's bed, but I wasn't really focused on anything besides getting her here ASAP. *What was the glass for?* There wouldn't even be that much in the house to take…Mom and Dad, trying to avoid the substance abuse problems that plagued their parents, decided when they got married that there would be no alcohol in their home. There aren't really any drugs either, and the only pills we have are Lana's laxatives and then the normal stuff: Tylenol, Benadryl, and the like.

But it's not like those are harmless, and another sob racks me as I think back to Health class on the day we covered overdoses. Enough of any of those could be fatal. Lana, I hope you didn't...

I'm back to uncontrollable bawling when Mandy comes back in.

"Hey," she says. "Are you ok?"

I ignore her question and answer with another. "How is she?"

"Better," she says with a smile. "She's awake and talking a little."

Relief floods over me.

"Do you know what happened?"

"Well, we're still running some tests," Mandy says. "But it's looking like she was suffering from exhaustion coupled with some pretty serious anemia."

So she wasn't trying to kill herself. Well, at least all at once.

"Can I see her?" I ask, grabbing a tissue and dabbing my eyes.

"Yeah," Mandy says. "I'll take her to you."

She doesn't have to tell me twice. I jump up and follow her out the door, rushing to see my sister.

Lana is sitting up, supported by the incline bed. She is attached to what I'm guessing is a heart monitor and a bunch of other machines I don't recognize. She's got IVs running in and out of her, and her paper-thin frame is somehow made tinier by the hospital gown.

Seeing me eye her attire, she laughs faintly. "Sexy, right? This thing has less coverage than a cell phone in Montana."

I smile. My sister is back.

Thank God.

"What happened?" I ask, dragging a chair from the edge of the room.

"I just forgot to eat supper, that's all," she says with a shrug.

Yeah. She forgot. Kind of like how she forgot to eat lunch, too. And breakfast. And about every other meal for the past few years.

"Anyway," she says. "I should be good to leave here soon."

"Two hours ago you were passed out on your bed," I say, skeptically.

"It's ok," she says.

It's not ok. It's so not even close to ok. Lana is killing herself, and I'm too much of a sissy to confront her about it.

"And I'm sorry," she says, reaching her tube-filled hand to hold mine.

"What the hell are *you* sorry for?" I ask, incredulously. "*I'm* sorry."

"I'm sorry I scared you, and I'm sorry I put you through this," she says. "I'm such an idiot."

"I'm the idiot," I say. "I screamed at you, I tore you to shreds and I knew you weren't…doing the best and I still crucified you."

"Yeah," Lana says. "But I deserved it."

"No you didn't," I counter. "No one deserves to have their own sister treat them so horribly."

"Yeah," she says, with a bitter laugh. "Well, right back at you."

"I didn't mean like that!" I say.

"I know you didn't. It's ok. It really is. I would've been really pissed, too."

She pauses.

"Besides, you had some pretty good lines in there. You ought to consider becoming a writer."

I give her a wary look. She grins.

"That's not funny," I say.

"Yeah, it is," she replies.

"Just promise me one thing. Please," I gesture to all the machinery she is currently hooked up to. "Don't let this happen again."

She looks at me with a weak smile. "It won't."

Yeah, right.

She and I talk for another half and hour or so. Mom and Dad call us back frantically, and Lana takes the phone, smoothly explaining away the whole "so out-of-it Morgan had to carry me into the ER" incident as nothing more than a forgotten meal. They fall for it hook, line and sinker, and she even convinces them that they don't need to leave New York early. It's actually kind of impressive, and my heart drops a little lower with every word that comes out of her mouth.

It's almost three in the morning, and all my adrenaline from earlier has worn off. Unfortunately, I'm Lana's and my ride home. I'm running on whatever you have left after you've run out of fumes, and Mandy takes me to get coffee.

"You really had me worried there, kid," she says as she hands me the piping hot cup. "I've never seen you cry before."

Yeah. My pain tolerance is legendary around here. You know when they ask you to rate your discomfort on a level from 1 to 10? The highest I've ever gone was three, and that was when I dislocated my shoulder falling down the stairs at school during 6th grade lunch. In front of everyone.

"She just scared me, that's all," I say.

"It's ok to be scared," she says. "It shows you care."

Her pager goes off, and she runs off, leaving me with my mug of coffee walking gingerly back toward Lana's room. No need to add third-degree burns to my list of embarrassing injuries.

Just as I'm about to head inside, I hear a voice inside that doesn't belong to my sister. I lean up against the door and listen.

"Well," says the voice, a deep male baritone, "I'm sure this isn't shocking to you, but there were no drugs in your system."

Any last shred of doubt I had about this not being a suicide attempt vanishes. This was Lana hurting herself all right…but at least she wasn't going for the ultimate self-destruction.

"You're not anemic…kind of. You've got most of the vitamins, and folic acid and such but you're missing protein. Do you take vitamins?"

"No," Lana says, and as far as she knows she's telling the truth.

Damn. How did I manage to *help* her pull off not eating? I should have just called her fat myself.

"Still, your blood sugar, blood pressure and heart rate were all really low," he says. "It's a good thing your sister found you when she did."

Lana doesn't answer. Maybe this will serve as a wake-up call. If this doesn't, what will?

"Either way," he says. "I'd like to keep here overnight at least and maybe for a few days just to be safe."

I'm all for this idea. I don't want to out Lana. I don't want to share her secret. But I don't think she could keep up the charade under medical supervision for more than 48 hours without collapsing again or somebody putting the pieces together.

Lana is, for obvious reasons, dead set against this idea.

"Look," she says, her weak voice getting a little bit stronger. "I'm awake. I'm oriented. I can sit up without any alarms going off now, and I feel a hundred times better than I did. And," she adds, realizing she has one more weapon in her arsenal, "I'm 19."

Since Lana is legally an adult, they can't force her to stay, and she knows it.

The voice I'm assuming belongs to her doctor knows it too, and he relents.

"Ok," he says. "But I'm going to set up an appointment for you with a GP and a nutritionist."

"Fine," she says. I know she has no intention of going, but she's doing a fairly good job of making him think she's gung-ho about it.

I decide now is a good time to enter and I push open the door, saying, "Hi, sis!"

Lana smiles, and the figure in scrubs turns around.

I almost pass out myself. Good Lord, is he attractive.

I force myself to focus beyond those gorgeous baby blue eyes, though, even as they look into mine and say, "You must be Morgan."

"That's me," I say, carefully getting a one-handed grip on the coffee before shaking his outstretched hand. He's got a firm grip, and I catch a glimpse of his incredibly toned biceps. Why can't he be ten years younger? (Or me ten years older?)

"We can head home soon, sis," Lana says, clearly daring the super hot doctor to stop her.

"…After you sign some forms, get those appointments set up and we get those out of you," he says, pointing at the IVs still dripping into my sister's arm. "We'll let the bags run out and you'll be free to go, alright?"

"Ok," Lana says, not pushing her luck.

Super Hot Doc turns to me.

"I'll take you to get started on the paperwork, ok?" he says.

He leads me out to the mostly empty waiting room and grabs some forms off the counter on the way there. We sit down and I look in vain for a place to set my mostly empty coffee cup. He takes it for me and sets in on an end table.

"So," he says. "You're the Morgan we've been hearing so much about."

"I guess," I say with a smile as I try to remember the name of our health insurance.

"She was saying what a great sister you are," he said. "Bringing her in like that."

"What are sisters for?" I respond, trying to control the sweat pooling under my arms. I really need new deodorant.

"So, are you a student here in town?" he asks. "She's lucky you're around."

"Yeah," I say, skipping the box for Lana's social security number. Like I even know mine.

"What year?" he asks.

"Sophomore," I respond. "Halfway there!"

He laughs, showing perfectly white, straight teeth. He's like McDreamy, but younger.

"Are you good to drive?" he asks.

"What do you mean?" I ask. "I'm awake, if that's what you mean."

"No," he says. "I mean, I get that you drove here because you had no choice, but are you good alcohol-wise?"

"What?" Now I'm really lost.

"I'm guessing by that very cute dress by the way," he says, without a hint of sarcasm. "That you were out clubbing before you got home?"

"Um…Winter Formal," I say sheepishly. "You get that I'm her *younger* sister, right?"

"Oh," he says, eyes widening, backtracking as fast as he can. "Oh. I'm…I'm so sorry…I thought you were a *college* sophomore!"

It's all I can do not to do a little happy dance. Not only is Super Hot Doc hitting on me, but he thinks I'm old enough for that not to be creepy!

It doesn't take long to get everything arranged, and I make sure I have the dates of Lana's appointments so she can't conveniently "lose" them. We head out to the parking lot, and I use the very last of my energy to drive us home. Lana falls asleep almost as soon as we get in the car. Super Hot Doc (whose name is actually Jerod) told me she probably would, and I wake her up when we pull in the garage. We both drag ourselves out of the SUV and head inside, ready for the sleep we both desperately need.

Chapter 11:

"Little darling/it's been a long cold lonely winter," –The Beatles, Here Comes The Sun

I awake with a start again, my bladder about to explode.

I really need to stop drinking beverages before bed.

I stand up, only to be confused. What am I doing on Lana's floor in my more-valuable-than-Laverne dress?

Ignoring this question to attend to more pressing matters, I run into Lana's bathroom and heed the call of nature.

As I'm sitting there, the details slowly begin to come back. Winter Formal. Lana passing out. The hospital. Coffee. Jerod the Super Hot Doc.

I smile at the thought of that last part.

As soon as I'm done in the bathroom, I go back to check on Lana. Jerod had said she'd probably sleep like a baby, but he doesn't know my sister and after last night I'm not taking any chances.

Lana is asleep, but her color is ten shades brighter than last night. Just to be sure, I creep toward my sleeping sister and gently place my hand over her delicate ribcage, afraid if I apply any pressure I'll snap her in two. Her chest rises and falls, up and down, up and down. So far, so good. I reach down for her wrist, searching for the rhythm that will make me stop worrying and go back to sleep. I'm not entirely sure what I'm doing, but I try to copy what George Clooney does on ER and sure enough, I find it. It beats like a metronome –slow, but not too slow, and steady.

Breathing my own sigh of relief, I quietly creep off to my own room to change into sweats and grab a pillow and a few blankets to make Lana's floor a little less uncomfortable. Ringo follows behind me, somehow knowing that now is not a good time to start barking.

I sneak back into Lana's room and lay down on the floor next to her bed, with Ringo curled up right beside.

Lana and I both finally drag our butts out of bed around 11:30, when Ringo's "I need to pee" barks begin to be too loud to ignore. I let Ringo outside before he turns Lana's lamppost into a fire hydrant and slowly head toward the pantry. As I pull open the doors, Lana comes down the stairs.

"Good morning," she says.

"Good morning," I say, happy to see her up and about. "Um…how about breakfast?"

She smiles. "Sure."

Wow. That was easier than expected.

"What sounds good?" I ask, eager to get her to actually eat.

"Those aren't really Wheaties, are they?" she asks, pointing at the cereal I'm pouring out of the orange box with the really toned athlete on the front.

"Frosted Flakes," I say. Dad and I, despite all our troubles, have an arrangement when it comes to cereal. Mom freaks out if the food in our pantry is not organic, made from whole grain and bares an extreme resemblance to cardboard, and Dad and I came up with the Wheaties scheme when I was nine. We were hungry and watching *The Sting*, back when he still had time for Morgan-Dad movie nights. Of course, now the only time I see Dad is during family dinners and when he and Lana have a premiere, but the Wheaties have remained a sacred secret. Do not separate that man from his Frosted Flakes.

"I'll have a bowl of those," she says, taking a dish out of the cupboard.

"I'll get the milk," I say, grabbing the whole milk carton. (It's actually 1%. I've been switching the labels for months now. It's been so long since Lana actually drank milk she can't tell the difference.)

Lana balks at the idea of this incredibly fattening accompaniment to her bowl of sugar-bombs, and heads to the fridge for the 1%.

Ha. Hook, line and sinker.

She serves herself a decent sized portion, and I can barely contain my smile at the sound of the cereal falling into the bowl. Granted, my pile of corn-sugar-bliss towers over hers, but I, like my father, need Frosted Flakes to live. Come between me and Tony the Tiger, and I will haunt your dreams.

We eat in silence, me chowing down like a five-year-old and Lana taking slow, delicate bites, like after all this time she's forgotten how to chew and swallow. She does finish, though, and she puts her empty bowl in the sink. It's not much –but it's something, and I'll take it in a heartbeat.

Lana goes to the living room and I hear the TV turn on, followed by the voice of the *Crime Stories* narrator. My sister is a sucker for good drama.

Knowing her butt will not be leaving the couch until she knows who murdered the cheating millionaire husband who was embezzling from his company, abusing his wife and blackmailing a government official, I decide I can leave her. I'm about to head upstairs to take a shower when the phone rings. It's Dad. Goodie.

"Hello?" I answer, with minimal enthusiasm.

"Morgan?" Dad says. "Hey, how is Lana doing?"

"Fine," I say. "We both just got up."

"Based on the TV in the background, she's watching *Crime Stories*?"

"Yep."

"Filthy rich husband with a trophy wife, a mistress and a mean streak?"

"Gosh, how did you know?" I ask, sarcastically. Actually, he stole the words right out of my mouth. I hate it when he does that.

"Listen," he says. "Can you run downstairs and grab a phone number for me? I left it on my desk and I need to get ahold of them ASAP."

"Ok." Whatever to make this conversation end.

"It's on a purple sticky note. Marshall Downs is the name. Just text me the number when you find it," he says, as I start heading toward the stairs. "Can you hand the phone to Lana?"

"Yeah," I say. "Ok. Bye."

"Bye," he says, and I hand the phone off to Lana before heading downstairs and into Dad's office.

I don't come down here unless I have to, and after stepping in I remember why. The place looks like my room, but worse, if that's possible. There are papers in disarray, office supplies scattered without care, and, oddly enough, a can of Spam sitting on top of the filing cabinet. The only things that sit looking like they are in the right place are the neatly labeled, empty organizers that are supposed to be holding the office supplies, invoices and various important documents.

It's going to take forever to find this stupid phone number. There are sticky notes everywhere, and I about trip over another stack of paper as I take a few more cautionary steps into the office.

Avoiding more piles of paper, magazines and reviews, I finish the obstacle course that is my father's office, throwing myself into the relatively safe swivel chair. Mentally preparing myself to face the onslaught of chaos, I turn the seat to take on The Desk.

It's The Desk because that's how things are around the Tannunbum house. Mail for Dad? Put it on The Desk. Missed call from some important person? Take a message and leave it on The Desk. Still young and stupid enough to actually want to spend time with your father? Put a request on The Desk and he might actually get back to you.

I start rifling through the papers, searching for a purple sticky note. I'm finding invoices, bills and emails, but no sign of a phone number.

After about thirty seconds of continuous searching, I stumble across a folder. It's not what I'm looking for, but I hold it out in my hands and just stare at it, debating.

The file is labeled "The Manuscript Formerly Known as Scrambled Eggs".

Do I open it?

Do I put it away and pretend I never saw it?

Hell, no.

I know this is immoral. I get that I'm violating my father's privacy and this is not the sort of action a good girl like me is supposed to take. But hey, he left it out, right?

I fling it open…only to realize it's empty.

Wow. He's still messing with me, 1,000 miles away.

Deflated, I continue to search until I find the purple sticky note, only to have my heart sink a little further. The number is for Marshall Downs, of Marshall Investigative Services.

I am so, so screwed.

Chapter 12:

"Let it Be/Let it Be/Let it Be/There will be an answer/let it be," –The Beatles, *Let it Be*

Lana and I sleep into the afternoon on Sunday, me rising only for food and she after I drag her out of bed. Although it's after one, I still feel like my first meal of the day should be of the breakfast variety and pour myself a bowl of Frosted Flakes. Lana follows suit, her serving still tiny but bigger than that of the day before. Progress. I like it.

As we sit down to eat, I turn to her to ask a question.

"How did you get it?"

"Get what?" she says, heading to the fridge for milk.

"*Scrambled Eggs.*"

She shoots me a wary look.

"I'm not going to yell at you again, I promise. I just can't figure out how you got it to Avery. The one hard copy had notes written in the margins."

"Simple," she says. "I'm the one who bought you Laverne, remember?"

"So you hacked me?" I ask, horrified and a little impressed at the same time.

"No," she says. "But I did remember how it was set up, and your password wasn't too difficult to guess."

"It's 21 characters long!" I say indignantly, counting out the letters on my fingers.

"Which would be hard to hack," Lana replies with a small smile. "…if those 21 characters were not TheLongAndWindingRoad."

Oh. I guess I could've made it a smidge more difficult than my favorite song. But there's no way Dad could guess that password. He does know I like the Beatles; he's the one who turned me on to them. But I've tried to hide my love for the Fab Four from him for a few years simply so he doesn't get the satisfaction of being right, so he probably thinks I've moved on to Ke$ha or something. Gag.

"But you didn't tell Dad any of it, right?" I ask.

"No," she says. "That's between you and him. I'm staying out of it."

So much for asking her to help me keep him off my tail. But at least she won't be telling him either. I'm actually in a better spot than I was last week – I know who sent it, I know how they got it and I know Dad doesn't know any of it. So far, so good.

Maybe I can pull this off after all.

Lana and I sleep the rest Sunday away, our internal clocks still off from our Friday night/Saturday morning adventure. Before I know it, it's Monday and I'm sitting in Geography, looking as bleary-eyed as everyone else.

After Mr. Rooney finishes up the announcements, Mr. O'Malley says good morning and starts to hand out a sheet of paper titled "Traditional Taxation Methods", announcing in a ridiculously happy tone, "Group projects, everyone!"

Everyone groans internally, although a few can't contain their disappointment and accidently mutter the sound aloud. Group projects are awful. You end up working your butt off for a grade you'll be sharing with someone else, and unless you're lucky enough to pick your groups you'll probably end up with a bunch of slackers who will make you do the whole thing for them.

"I'll be assigning partners this time around," he continues.

Ok. God, are You punishing me for snooping around on Dad's desk?

Mr. O'Malley finally gets to the back of the room in counting off, and I am the second number twelve. I get up and start searching for my counterpart, praying it's Rebekkah or Emilee or even Eleanor. Just please not…

"So, are you the other number twelve?" Sierra asks.

Oh, yeah. I'm totally being punished.

"So, what are we doing?" Sierra asks. Again.

"We're making a PowerPoint on the Consumption Tax."

"So, like, on alcohol?"

Someone shoot me. Please.

"No," I say, being as patient as I can. "It's the concept of being taxed on what you buy."

"Whatever," she says, with a wave of her hand. I don't know why on earth this child is in an AP class. My school has zero standards for taking honors courses, and she got in as easy as I did, despite once giving a very persuasive speech on saving the country of Africa.

I will totally end up doing this entire project. Just what I need right now. I can't trust Sierra to write her own name correctly, let along create an adequate analysis of a controversial (and very boring) taxation technique. Unless it involves Snooki, shopping or a hot guy, she's not interested. Period.

It might just be faster, actually, if I do the whole thing myself. Sierra is already texting away under the desk, totally unfocused on the presentation we need to start working on. I don't give her enough credit. She does have skills after all, at least in the electronic-device-concealing department.

I sigh. This is going to be a long, long Monday.

My next two classes do not go any better. In Spanish, I nearly fall asleep when we review the present perfect tense for the thousandth time. Health is not an improvement either –I sit by myself (again), awkwardly trying to find a partner for the Heimlich maneuver demonstration we all have to do to pass. I end up with one of the wrestlers, who fails to remember he is supporting my weight and promptly sends me crashing as soon as Mr. Cummings declares the demo is over. I land straight on my butt and the entire class laughs. Awesome.

By the time I get to lunch, I've about had enough. The 8-hour nap I took through most of yesterday afternoon meant I got about zilch sleep yesterday night, tossing and turning and terrified I was turning into Lana. I'm tired, I'm stressed, and my ass hurts. Oh, and it's only 5th period.

If Katie were still here, I'd rip into my day and she'd have me laughing at my incredibly sore coccyx in five minutes flat. But Katie isn't here, and I am. Which blows, frankly. Because nothing is worse for me than lunch.

Now, before you go all "Oh, so she's got food issues, too" on me, know this: my absolute hatred of lunch doesn't have anything to do with food. Our cafeteria's fare is – edible, actually, for the most part, although we do occasionally run into U.F.O.'s.

(Unidentified Food Objects. If you can't name what it is within 5 seconds of looking at it, you probably shouldn't be stuffing it in your mouth.) No, I hate lunch because of my lunch table.

It's a big old plastic model, with seven seats on each side. You'd think with 13 other people sitting there somebody would notice I exist.

I always get stuck at the end. Always. Even if I'm like the third person to get the table, seats get saved for everyone else and I end up at the edge with my breaded chicken and fruit cup. No one knows I'm there. The people at my table don't even notice I'm gone. I was at a youth conference on improving human rights for three days and nobody said a word. These are some of my closest friends (other than Emilee and Rebekkah, who have lunch a different period) –and they don't seem to give a crap, at least when they're in the presence of other people. I'm ok to hang out with when I'm the only option, but once anyone else shows up, I'm toast.

See why I hate lunch?

Today is no exception to the "Morgan Doesn't Exist" rule, and even though I want desperately to rant about how much my day has sucked, I can't get a word in edgewise. They're all too busy discussing "Smashing Sunrise", the newest and final book in the "Evening" series, a ridiculously long chain of supernatural novels. Fantastic. Another conversation I have nothing to add to.

"I'm like, so sad Dmitri's dead!" Kaci exclaims.

"Well, he's not dead," Olivia implores. "He's like, in a coma. His soul is still there but his body is like, useless."

"That's such a waste of a six-pack of abs!" Eleanor says, jumping it.

"But like, didn't the Wamps take out all his blood?" asks Sophie.

"What the hell is a Wamp?" I ask myself, realizing too late I've said it out loud. Of course, the one time I don't want people to listen to what I'm saying, they all do, my question hanging in open silence. My friends all turn and stare at me, shocked, primarily, to see there is indeed a person sitting there, and also that that person doesn't know the answer to this inquiry.

"Werewolf-Vampire hybrid," they say in unison, before turning back to each other.

74

"So, like, Dmitri kills himself in like, an attempt to determine his own destiny or something?" Kaci says.

"Kinda," replies Olivia. "Remember that part back in "Fresh Lunar"?"

These are awful names for novels. Just saying.

Olivia continues undaunted, saying, "…Dmitri takes the poison in order to protect his inner spirit from the Wamps and Zombie Queens…"

I stopped listening at "Zombie Queens". And why are these characters always named "Dmitri", anyway?

When Sophie is done with her rant, I try again to enter the conversation.

"Guys, you wouldn't believe what happened last period…"

I don't get any further. Not a single one hears me, too lost in their own happy little worlds to see I'm miserable in mine. I was kind of hoping they would finally listen, but I should've known they wouldn't. Still, I am more disappointed than I thought I would be.

I pick up my tray and head over to the trash can, dumping my wrapper and empty milk cartoon. I set the tray down on the counter and head up the stairs to the bathroom. Opening the door, I step inside and head into the only stall with a functioning lock. Using the metal contraption, I shut the door and begin the painful 10 minute wait for the period to end. It's better to sit in here than stand alone in the lobby. At least nobody can see me in here. I pull my phone out and start playing PacMan. I'm up to level 6 before it begins.

"It" is the onslaught of teenage girls who always invade the bathroom after lunch. Some are checking their makeup, some are actually using the restroom and others are just talking. For some reason, relieving one's bladder is a group activity for high school females. No one goes to the bathroom by themselves. They come in waves, none sticking around long enough to notice one stall never seems to vacate. I've learned a *ton* since I've started hiding out in here. There is no better way to stay up on the latest gossip.

Girls come and go, complaining about P.E. make-ups and boys and talking about what crazy thing some freshman did when she got a little too drunk at a party. Nothing makes my ears perk up, and I keep running away from the ghosts out to eat my little round PacMan.

Over the next few minutes, the bathroom starts to empty. I really should get going; class starts in a few minutes. I start to put my legs back down on the floor, but see something that makes me pause. Someone wearing a pair of shiny, beaded silver Converse –the kind I've always wanted but never dared to try to pull off –has entered the bathroom alone. No one does that. Well, except maybe me. Have I found a kindred spirit?

Any hopes of finding another human being lame enough to be hiding out in the bathroom playing a video game, however, are dashed. Sparkly Shoes, whoever she is, has gone into the bathroom next to me and is hurling her lunch. And probably her breakfast, too.

The sound alone is making me gag. Poor thing probably tried the Mystery Meat. I want to speak up and ask if she's ok, but then it dawns on me. She doesn't know I'm here. Not wanting to add to my list of Awkward Moments of the day (what if she thinks I'm spying on her?), I wait for Sparkly Shoes to leave before sneaking out of the bathroom to slide into Study Hall just in time.

As soon as the bell hits 3:15, I throw on my backpack and head straight for the FDR High pool. There's never anybody here after school, which is just what I need.

Despite all my struggles with coordination on land, I actually know what I'm doing in the water. I love to dive in, smell the chlorine and just kick my legs and paddle my arms until I'm soaking wet, exhausted and not so frustrated anymore. I love being underwater, where there's no noise and no chaos, just me and my thoughts.

I head into the showers that double as storage space and unlock my locker, pulling out my black competition Speedo and a ponytail. Trying to contain my hair into one tie is more difficult than it probably should be, but the strands do eventually obey and I change into my swimsuit. It's the one-piece I wear for Swim Team, so it's not flattering at all – tight everywhere, and even tighter at all the wrong angles. It's not supposed to look good though…it's supposed to function, and that's all I really care about. It's better than a bikini by a long shot. Girls like Sierra, with toned abs and complete confidence, will strut these decks like they're Kim Kardashian and get all the guys to turn. I have a six-pack, too. I really do. It's just deep, deep in the fridge. And I, as made blatantly obvious by my super attractive Speedo, also have the breasts to fill out one of those little string creations.

But they're horrible for swimming, and what fun is doing a back flip off the diving board if you're worried you're about to flash anyone nearby? Besides, those girls would laugh mercilessly at how I look right now, with goggles on and hair looking like it's in a wrestling match with itself.

After standing in front of the mirror in vain, I come to the conclusion that I will not be able to turn my swimsuit into anything more attractive and head out toward the water. This is always my favorite part. There's no one around to tell me not to, and the deck is dry, so I back up and sprint toward the pool, jumping in with an incredibly satisfying splash. As soon as I'm in, I'm off, swimming across the water with the all the stress I've bottled up over the last couple of days. At first, I think about Lana, and *Scrambled Eggs*, and how I have no idea how to fix either of them. After a few laps around the pool, though, my mind just gives up, and my legs and arms move in sync as my brain goes completely blank.

Before I know it, it's an hour later, I'm more wrinkly than a prune, and I've burned off more frustration than I knew I was even holding. I hate to leave the water, though, and I do a dead man's float in the middle lane for ten more minutes, just to feel the pressure in my ears and total silence in the room.

Eventually, I realize that I have to get out at some point, and I slowly drag myself from the pool and head toward the showers, rinsing myself off and changing back into my street clothes. I leave my swimsuit to dry on a rack –no one's going to steal something that unattractive –and lock up my towel and goggles.

Heading out toward my car, I hurry quickly through the parking lot, the cold January wind whipping my still sopping wet hair. I'd have blown it dry, but I am no longer allowed to use bathroom stylizers without Lana's presence after what she likes to call "The Hairspray Incident". (How was I supposed to know you're not supposed to expose it to heat?)

Finally ready to face my family, I pull out of the FDR parking lot and head home, turning on my Beatles playlist for good measure. I pull into the garage a little while later, grabbing my backpack and heading inside.

Let the games begin.

Chapter 13:

"Love love me do/you know I love you/so please/love me do"-The Beatles, Love Me Do

"So how was New York?" Lana asks Dad, as she picks up the single duffle bag my father brought for the whole trip. The man travels light.

"Wonderful, dear," my mother says, breezing in the door as I try in vain to pull in her tote out of the back seat of our Mercedes. The other five pieces of much larger luggage are in the trunk, and I can barely get this tote off the ground to begin with. Why does she need this much stuff for three days?

"We raised almost five million for the shelter," Dad says, through the door.

At least one of those five came straight from him. My dad may be among the stingiest people on the face of the earth, but he's got a soft spot for charities.

"It'll hopefully keep them open for another few years," Mom says, yawning.

Dad, also showing signs of the five-hour flight, continues to go on about the shelter while I head back outside and pull out more of Mom's luggage. The pieces are strategically arranged, put inside the trunk just so in order to make everything fit. Unfortunately, the fit is a little too tight, and I can't even get my fingers in between the bags, let alone try to lift them out. I give it a few more tries, but my hands begin to protest the abuse, and I give up on the stupid luggage and head inside.

Dad is just wrapping up his speech on the socioeconomics of poverty as I step inside, still rubbing my fingers.

"…and that's why they're stuck in this rut. Anyway," he says, seeing me. "I think a low key night is what everyone needs."

"Agreed," Lana and I say in unison, praying that this means no family dinner.

"As for dinner," Dad says, right on cue. "I ate on the plane."

He looks to Mom.

"Still a little nauseous, dear," she says. "No food for me."

She's not nauseous. She just won't eat. Why do I even bother trying to get Lana to feed herself?

I head up to my room before my dad can change his mind, closing the door and locking it behind me.

Ahh. Peace.

I head over to Laverne, because I've come up with a bit of a hunch. Maybe the reason Dad can't figure out that *Scrambled Eggs* is mine is because it's not as obvious as I think it is. I haven't actually read the manuscript since I finished it six months ago, and maybe I'm just remembering things worse than they are. That would explain a lot, actually. Maybe I only put a few things from my real life in there. What if Lana only caught it because we're really close and tell each other almost everything? Maybe other than the remarkable similarity in names, Meagan Tatum seems like a totally functional, completely normal human being –in other words, not me.

There's only one way to find out if the delusion I'm working up is actually plausible, and I put in the password to Laverne. Taking in a gulp of air, I open up *Scrambled Eggs* and start to read.

Oh no. I am sooo not remembering things worse than they are.

When I first started reading, I cringed every time I read something that came from my real life. After about twenty minutes, I realized it was just faster to stay in a permanent state of angst, and the hits have just kept coming.

Everything in *Scrambled Eggs* comes from my life. Everything.

The main character, Meagan, lives in a three-story house in an L.A. suburb with her writer father, brilliant sister and retired mother. She hollows out books to hide her junk food, has a pug named after one of the less attractive Beatles, and has also given her laptop/printer duo an 80's sitcom-inspired moniker. She goes to a school with an incredibly pathetic mascot, has a favorite English teacher named Mrs. Kayle and has to deal with super annoying Populars.

Anything sound familiar?

I'm so, so, so screwed. I described everything in my life in those 200 pages. I wrote about the fireplace mantel, The Desk, and even the spitballs on my ceiling, and that's just the house. I'm pretty sure I could pass *Scrambled Eggs* off as my diary –if people's diaries usually come with cinematography suggestions written in. Seriously, how does Dad not know this is mine?

Maybe he does. How could he not? That would mean he's just screwing with me. Or he's just completely oblivious. That wouldn't surprise me. It's not like the man has shown any interest in me after realizing –newsflash–I'm more him than I am Mom. Once his career took off, it was either writing or directing or Lana. No time for Morgan, the one who once got a concussion in gym class by standing up into an open locker. Actually, I guess that happened to Meagan, too. Why did I have to put so much of my life in there?

So I guess I'm stuck between a rock and…well, another rock. And possibly a third rock. Because Mom might be reading it, too.

Awesome. I'm up for family member of the year over here. I've written a manuscript about how terrible the people I live with are, and somehow that manuscript found its way into their hands –and they love it because they're too uninvolved to get that they're the parents I'm criticizing mercilessly.

Great.

My head is spinning from all the ways in which my world will blow to smithereens if Dad finds out, and I stand up from my desk, lock down Laverene and head downstairs to get some water. I'd just grab something from my stash up here, but caffeine and I at 9:00 pm don't get along well, and I need something to clear my head.

My brain continues to go through every possibility as I slowly head down the stairs. What if Dad does know and he's just messing with me? Wouldn't he be really pissed though? I mean, if he really knew that he was Mitchell Tatum? But still…maybe that empty folder was him screwing with me. If so, it's about time I started firing back. Actually, firing back is probably a good plan no matter if he knows or not. If he does, he gets the crap he deserves for putting me through this and if he doesn't, it'll throw him off my trail, which is perfect.

I'm almost to the kitchen, and he's sitting there, reading what I'm guessing is *Scrambled Eggs*. Of course.

I almost turn around and run back upstairs, but I'm pretty sure he's seen me and I don't want to cast any suspicion on myself. Pretending his presence hasn't made my heart rate double, I nonchalantly walk to the fridge and pour myself a glass of water. I'm about to make my escape when he speaks up.

"Morgan," he says.

"Yeah?" I say, trying to sound as bored and un-terrified as possible.

"You named your laptop and printer, right?" he says.

Uh-oh.

"What?" I say.

Crap. Crap. Crap. Crap.

"Didn't you like, name them Cagney and Lacey?"

"No," I say, hoping he'll leave it at that.

"But they do have names, right?" he asks, staring at me through his reading glasses.

"Yeah," I say, hoping my next fib won't come back to bite me. "EVERYBODY names them. It's a thing. Mine are Laverne and Shirley."

"Right," he says with a smile. "Whoever wrote this went with Richie and Fonzie."

"Nice," I say, heading toward my room as fast as I can without it looking like I'm trying to flee. I'm almost up the stairs when I have a sudden thought, the first attack of Operation Save My Hide in my head.

"Oh," I say, sounding as off-handed as I can. "This Marshall guy called. He said he's 'made progress'," I make air quotes. "On something to do with that movie. What's it called? Deviled Eggs? Anyway, I wrote it down and stuck it in one of the piles by your desk. Goodnight!"

I head up to my room with a smile. That ought to stall him for a while. I'm sure the Marshall guy did call. Sometime. Probably. But Dad's office is so cluttered he'll search and search and never find the "message", and he'll still chalk it up to his horrendous organization skills.

Looks like I may have tied the score, at least for now.

Bring it on, old man.

It's 9 a.m, and I could use a serious caffeine jolt.

I spent all last night trying to come up with a plan to further derail Dad, but I came up with absolutely nothing, despite brainstorming until 2 a.m. Sleeping on the problem provided no further results, and now it's second period and I'm stuck with Sierra on our ridiculous taxation project, which is not doing my tired brain any favors. I'm busy creating an MLA format bibliography while Sierra, who hasn't even bothered to log on to her computer, fingers through a copy of *Our Town*. It's required reading for Slacker English, and Sierra looks about as excited to be reading it as I am to be sitting next to her. A loose leaf sheet of paper lies in front of her, what appears to be a short essay entitled "The Theme of Our Town".

I start to read through Sierra's attempt at literature analysis out of the corner of my eyes, more so to keep myself awake than anything else. This ought to at least be entertaining. The following composition, written in a painfully fluorescent pink, lies in front of me:

"The theme of Our Town is really simple. Thornton Wilder wanted us to appreciate living in modern times where there are actually things to do, like Facebook. He wanted to remind the world how horrible things were in little Podunk towns in Maine, where nobody could do anything but talk to people and read. READ. And they didn't have anything in Elmo's Corners, not even any real horses or dishes or food. They had to just pretend. That's really sad. In conclusion, Thornton Wilder wanted all us people in the modern world to think about how deprived people were in the 1990's."

I try to stifle my giggles, but I can't keep a few from escaping, and Sierra looks up from her book and grabs the paper defensively.

"What are you laughing at?" she asks, in a sneer.

"Oh, nothing." I say, suppressing a grin. "But just FYI, you've got a few things wrong."

"Like what?" she says, rolling her eyes.

"It's set in the early 20th century, for starters."

"I got that right," she says indignantly, her trademark snottiness returning quickly. "I said 1990's."

"That's not all," I say, struggling further to maintain my composure after her last remark. "I've made this mistake a few times, too…it's actually in New Hampshire."

"Ok," she says. "Little state with lighthouses. Same dif."

"And you have the wrong Muppet."

"The wrong what?"

"The wrong Muppet."

"What the hell is a Muppet?"

"It's Grover's Corners, not Elmo's. And you don't really have the theme right."

"Ugh!" She crumples up the paper and throws it down in disgust. "That was my third try. This is such a stupid book."

"Play," I correct, although I know I should just shut up.

She rolls on as if I haven't spoken. "Why is Mrs. Wilkerson making us read this anyway? It's so pointless!"

Luckily for us, Mr. O'Malley has, up until this point, been outside the room and hasn't heard Sierra's outburst or been present to notice that we are both horribly off track. As Sierra continues to rant, however, he walks into the computer lab doors, just in time to hear her proclaim that small towns are stupid.

"Are we on task?" he says, approaching us.

"Yes," Sierra says, hitting a few keys on her keyboard to reveal she was logged on after all.

"Totally."

"Completely."

"Absolutely."

She and I continue to throw out adverbs until he moves on, leaving us with a few quizzical glances. As soon as his attention has shifted to a few boys logged on to Facebook, she turns to me.

"So…are you almost done? Cuz I have things to do."

I stare at her blankly, not opening my mouth for fear of what might come out.

"Oh…" she continues, smiling at me and pointing to the floor at her crumpled essay. "Could you like, throw that away?"

"Thanks!" she adds, not giving me a chance to answer.

Thankfully for her, the bell rings before I can explode on her. Not wanting to fight this battle, I pick up the horrendous essay and am about to throw it in the trash when something stops me.

This might be perfect.

Here's the thing. My father is desperate to read anything I write. Anything. The man practically salivates when it's my turn to make the grocery list. He wants to have an heir to his talents so badly that he'll read anything I've come up with to see if I've inherited his genius. Of course, since I don't let him read any of my real stuff, he has no idea I kind of did. Ish. The fact that I go to public school has not made this any easier. (His idea; apparently this experience will "make me a better person".) Budget cuts have slammed my school, and they've had to let a few teachers go. This makes our class sizes even larger, which means Parent-Teacher conferences only happen when a child is "struggling" simply so the teachers don't go insane. I may have bombed a test every once and a while, but I've never "struggled", and so Dad has never actually met Mrs. Kay, or Mrs. Wilkerson, or the other English teachers I've somehow managed to impress. This has made my dad even hungrier to read my work, and I've caught him looking in my textbooks at my worksheets or any other sliver of my writing I've been careless enough to leave lying around. He'll read anything he thinks is mine –including a really, really crappy lit analysis essay.

I straighten out the crumpled sheet and stick it in my bag on the way up to Spanish, stopping only to write my name in the top left-hand corner. I don't think I could have forced myself to write something like this, with the misspelled 2nd grade vocab words and missing punctuation. But it's so un-me and therefore un-Meagan that it might create some doubt in his mind, maybe convince him he's crazy for thinking his daughter could have written *Scrambled Eggs*, if that's what he thinks. If he doesn't think I wrote the movie, it's no harm, no foul, and he'll be even less likely to suspect me later. It's not the greatest nor most grammatically correct Trojan Horse the world has ever seen, but it's a start, and I know for sure if I leave it out he will read it.

Now starting to feel as though I may finally have the upper hand, I sit down in Spanish with a smile. It's even more perfect because he won't talk to me about it because I'll leave it in a place where he'll see it but will feel like he's snooping when he looks, like sticking it out of a folder on the kitchen counter. I'll have to transfer it to another sheet —Seirra's handwriting is far too girly for even my father to believe is mine and I would shoot myself before using such an atrocious shade of pink —but that shouldn't be too difficult. I need something to keep me occupied during the last ten minutes of Health anyway. Seriously, what is so hard about 30 compressions, two breaths, repeat?

    I know I'll need a stronger plan later, but that's ok. I at least have a second step in Operation Save My Hide, complete with hilariously awful lit analysis and poor grammar to boot.

    Let's see you top that, Dad.

Chapter 14:

"I wanna hold your hand" –The Beatles, I Wanna Hold Your Hand

As soon as I get home from school, I nonchalantly plant the fake *Our Town* essay on the kitchen counter. Leaving just enough of it sticking out of my English book, which I've lugged home solely for the purpose of tricking Dad, I throw it and a few other textbooks down and run up to my room. Ha. Let the magic begin.

Unfortunately, I really don't have much time to watch said magic. It's Tuesday, and that means it's Food Shelf night. When Katie still lived here, she and I would spend a few hours at the food bank sorting donations twice a month. When Katie left, I didn't want to stop helping, but I couldn't handle the massive piles of macaroni and cheese, canned creamed corn or baby formula by myself. Lana saw my need and pitched in, and now every other Tuesday she and I head over to the Marquette Food Pantry for a couple of hours before I have speech practice.

I only have about 10 minutes before Lana and I need to leave, and I yell out her name as I grab my stuff for speech. The Food Shelf is across town, and depending on the number of donations to sort, there's not always time to come back to grab my stuff. I run through the list of what I need: script? Check. Sheet music? Check. Protein bar, orange, water bottle and Reese's Cups? Check, check and check. I always sit down for a quick bite to eat before Lana and I need to leave to drive to the school. Lana always says she'll eat when she gets home. I'm sure she *totally* does.

As I'm grabbing the last of my items, Lana herself peeks in the door. "Hey," she says, keys in hand and purse on shoulder. "You ready to go?"

"Yeah," I say, slinging my "I ♥ The Beatles" bag onto my back. "Let's roll."

It's not too long of a drive before we reach the Holy Trinity Church, home to our town's food shelf. Even though Marquette is right outside of L.A., it's relatively wealthy (at least it looks like it is) and it's kinda small. There are only 10,000 people here, but a whole lot more of them have trouble providing healthy foods for themselves than you'd think. Katie and I were floored how fast donations disappeared from the shelves when we first started coming here a few years ago. It's the perfect volunteer opportunity –Lana and

I have our own key, and usually we're the only ones here, other than a few college kids. That means no cameras, no drama and no people awkwardly trying to spend time with Lana, derailing any progress we would have made. If there are other people there, most of them don't know who she is. She's Lana From the Food Shelf, dressed in yoga pants and sneakers, not Lana Tannunbum, decked out in Armani. I think that's why she likes it. Besides, the food bank needs all the help it can get–there's never enough staff, funding or donations, especially when the economy goes south. The last few times the Shelf's been dangerously low on supplies, however, a mysterious donor has given them exactly what they need, down to the correct vegetables. I'm pretty sure Lana has something to do with it, although she's never admitted as such.

When Lana and I step into the main hallway of the church, we notice something radically different. There is food everywhere. Boxes line the walls, three or four high and miraculously staying put. Plastic sacks from grocery chains sit in front of the boxes, and the hallway that is usually a good ten feet across is now reduced to less than six.

"Woah," Lana says, looking in awe at the walls of food in front of us.

"I know," I say, smiling despite the fact that this means Lana and I will be here really late. "This is great!"

Just then, a head pokes out of the food shelf doors.

"Hey guys!" A familiar voice says. It's Justin, a student at UCLA who also helps out at the food shelf.

"Where'd all this come from?" Lana asks, still a little in awe. This donation is big enough to cover the full need for at least three weeks, if not four or even five.

"School drive," he says, wiping off his hands and stepping out into the hallway.

"A *school drive* did this?" I ask, incredulously. School drives usually produce only a few boxes at most.

"Apparently kids could get out of a detention if they brought food," he says.

Oh. Well, that explains it.

"Me and Will and a couple of other kids already took care of about half of it," Justin says, eying the hallway still loaded with food.

"This is only half of it?" Lana asks, mind now even more blown.

"Yeah," he says. "But make sure to check the expiration dates. The school didn't do that for us."

Ugh. I hate it when people donate expired food. I mean, I get it if you just forget to check the date, but purposely giving us groceries gone bad? You do understand that actual people are going to be eating this stuff, right? Poor people are actually still people. They don't want to eat sketchy looking tomato soup that expired three years ago any more than you do.

"Anyway," he says, loading his backpack up onto his shoulders. "I've got to go. I have class. Good luck!"

He heads out the door, leaving Lana and I with two and a half hours to unload, sort and shelve two to three weeks of food. This could be interesting.

Lana and I stare at the gigantic walls of donations.

"Where do we start?" she asks, still looking around.

"Um…here, I guess!" I say, grabbing a stepstool and retrieving one of the boxes off the top layer. Moving the stepstool over, I pull down a few more and Lana and I begin sorting.

We've got it down to a science. After fumbling with the busted lock on the Shelf door, we get the darn thing open and grab at least a dozen empty half-boxes, setting them down in the little open space left in the crowded hallway. Dragging the donations to opposite ends of the line of empty pallets, we open the cartons and fire away, calling out the names of the items we have to each other as we toss them across the room.

"Do you have the corn pallet?"

"Yep!"

The corn flies across the room and Lana sets it in the appropriate pallet.

"How about mixed vegetables?"

"I don't think we have one of those."

"OK, I'll start one."

And so it goes. Canned peas, dried mashed potato mixes and boxes of macaroni and cheese soar across the hallway as Lana and I slowly whittle down the gigantic pile of food. There are a few moments this active circus of flying nonperishable food items stops —when we need to replace an empty pallet and shelve the full one, or when we have to stop and ask each other whether or not Fruit By The Foot actually qualifies as fruit. But things are going pretty smoothly, until half an hour into the process when Lana looks up and says in a genuinely confused tone, "What the hell…?"

"What?" I say, looking up from the Instant Beefaroni package I'm searching for a date on.

"Why does this look so weird?" Lana she says, holding up a box of lasagna.

"I dunno," I say, although even from across the room I can tell something about it is off. The coloring seems faded, but it doesn't look like it's ever been opened. "Let me see it. Was there an expiration date?"

"No," she says, still looking over the box. "Just some random code."

She sends the box my way. I catch it, and as soon as it's in my hands I can tell there's something wrong. I can't quite put my finger on what exactly, though, and I turn the box over and over in my hands to find the cause of my uneasiness. I'm about to give up and just tell Lana to throw it away when I come across the code she was talking about. Etched in the top are a series of six numbers, seemingly a random jumble of numerical nonsense. Suddenly, I'm horrified to know exactly what they mean.

"Eww!" I yell, instinctively throwing the box across the room to Lana.

"What?" she says, holding the box.

"It's older than me!"

"What?" she asks, bewildered, looking back down at the box.

"It's older than me! It expired before I was born!"

"Eww!" she shrieks, chucking it my way. "Why did you throw it to me?"

I catch the disgusting box of ancient lasagna and toss it right back. "Why did you throw it to me?"

"I dunno!" she says, flinging the lasagna towards me. "I don't wanna touch it!"

"Well, neither do I !" I say, returning the appalling pasta back with a quick toss.

We throw the nasty expired box back and forth a few more times before I overshoot, the lasagna landing in the corner a good five feet behind Lana.

"There," I say, relieved to not be touching the box anymore.

"Good."

"Wonderful."

"Wait…" Lana says, turning to me. "Who's going to pick it up?"

We both glance anxiously at each other for a few seconds before coming up with an idea.

"Justin," we say in unison, and return to our work, after making a beeline to the bathroom to do some serious hand-washing.

We sort for a few minutes more, and before we know it we've got barely more than an hour before we need to leave for speech. Although we've made a serious dent in the pile, we're probably not even halfway done with the giant load of food, and my stomach is beginning to growl. I pull out my cell and hit Contacts.

"What are you doing?" Lana asks, now studying a can of Cream of Chicken soup.

"Ordering pizza," I say. "This is too much work for a protein bar to handle!"

Greg's isn't too far from here, and I know they deliver. I always keep a twenty in my Beatles bag in case of emergencies anyway, and I'm going to need the fuel if I want to survive both this and speech practice. I call in my order, my usual: a medium extra cheese pizza. I won't be able to eat the whole thing, but I always put the leftovers in the minifridge hidden underneath my bathroom counter. The guy on the phone tells me it'll be about twenty minutes, and I hang up, my mouth already beginning to salivate.

Of course, it's kind of hard to avoid thinking about food while sorting lots and lots of food, and my stomach is about ready to explode from hunger by the time the delivery guy pulls into the church parking lot. By this time, Lana and I have managed to sort another ten boxes, and it's looking like we might actually finish. I meet the delivery guy at the church door, thanking him immensely and tipping him almost three dollars. I step inside and open the box, smelling the glory that is fresh cheese, garlic and a crust thicker than my fingers. I sit down and quickly begin scarfing it down, knowing I can't take too long to eat or we won't finish. I'm so lost in the fantastic pizza I don't hear Lana when she quietly asks me something.

"What?" I say, mouth full of crust.

"Can I have a piece?"

"Oh," I say, shocked but pleasantly surprised. "Oh, oh my gosh, yeah! Yeah, totally!"

Lana looks sheepish. "It's just…well, it's been a while since I had Greg's, and I'm…kinda hungry!" she says, with a small smile as she realizes she is capable of admitting that as a human being, she wants food.

I pull the biggest slice of the pie and hand it to her as she scoots over towards me. She takes the piece into her tiny hands and slowly puts it up toward her mouth. Gingerly, she puts it between her teeth and bites.

"Oh," she says, as the cheesy goodness hits her tongue. "Oh, that's good. Oh, that's so *good*!"

She doesn't speak to me again for the next ten minutes, as she eats not only that slice of pizza but another one as well, slowly but surely downing an entire 600 calories.

I couldn't be prouder.

Chapter 15:

"Lucy in the Sky with Diamonds..." –The Beatles, Lucy in The Sky with Diamonds

The next few days go by in the Tannunbum house with relative ease, at least compared to the last week. There are no announcements of new movies to be made, no major discoveries towards the identity of the author unearthed, and no sisters collapsing on me. Life is relatively good.

Dad and I have appeared to hit a stalemate. He hasn't made it any clearer if he knows the truth or not, and I haven't come up with any better plan of further derailing him. The "Our Town" essay trick did seem to work –after I got home from speech practice, I picked up my books and took them upstairs, hoping he'd already fallen for it. He had. The paper was in the book upside down. Hook, line and sinker, baby.

Things with Lana are also going pretty well. Over the last few days, I've managed to reintroduce her to the wonders that are macaroni and cheese, pb & j sandwiches and cookie dough ice cream. Granted, she only had a few noodles, maybe a third of the sandwich and only one spoonful of the ice cream (I made sure she got the biggest piece of cookie dough in the bowl), but we are making progress. There is color in my sister's cheeks, a shade of pink that can't be replicated by Cover Girl or Maybelline. I love it.

It's Friday (thank God), and I'm so ready for the weekend. We have LDE (Last Ditch Effort) practice for Speech tomorrow, which means I'll be out of the house all day. LDE practice is always the weekend before Districts, and it's either really fun or really stressful. If your group's not prepared (like Sophie's Musical Theatre team; they're on their third Glinda and still haven't found anyone who is both blonde and able to pull off the part), it sucks. If you're like my team and doing an incredibly bad show that was on Broadway for a total of two weeks, no one's familiar with the material and you can pretty much do whatever and no one will know the difference. We could run *The Robber Bridegroom* in our sleep; we'll be fine. Our Improv team is also totally prepared, which means I'll spend all day eating the pizza Mrs. Kay always orders and watching the events I won't be able to see at Districts. It's going to be a great Saturday –and best of all, I won't have to be at the dinner table when Dad brings up *Scrambled Eggs* again. I don't even have much homework –Sierra and I (and by that I mean I) finished the taxation project in class yesterday, and the only homework I have can wait until late Sunday night, when I'll finally force myself to do it.

Heading upstairs to my room, I toss my backpack at the foot of my bed and throw myself onto the mattress. Ah, sweet relaxation. Ringo jumps up to join me and snuggles in, nestling his head on my shoulder as my fan blows overhead. The whirling of the blades is about to put me to sleep when a scream permeates my near-slumber.

I nearly send Ringo crashing to the floor as I leap out of bed. There's only one person that sound could have come out of, and I fly out of my room and sprint across the hallway to Lana's room.

I burst in the door.

"Lana, what's wrong?" I ask, alarmed. I haven't heard her scream this loud since she found a snake in our garden.

"They don't fit!" she shrieks, throwing her favorite pair of skinny jeans across the room. "They don't fit!"

"Ok..." I say. I don't understand. Yeah, it's a hassle to go buy new jeans, especially if you're replacing your favorite pair, but if you're Lana and have designers clamoring to give you their clothes for free, I don't see why it's such a big deal.

"Don't you get it?" Lana says, tears begin to appear in her eyes. "They don't fit anymore. Don't you know what that means?" She collapses to floor in sobs.

"I knew I shouldn't have done it, I *knew*, damn it!" she says, now in a barely audible whisper.

"Shouldn't have done what?" I ask, sinking down to sit next to her.

"Eaten that pizza...oh, God, and the ice cream, and the peanut butter, and the jelly, oh God..." she says, staring down at her scrawny legs, poking out of her boy shorts like sticks. "Look!"

Now I understand. After a week of me forcing food down her throat, Lana has finally gained some weight. And now, she's going absolutely nuts.

Suddenly, Lana stops sobbing and tries to stand.

"Where are you going?" I ask, my sisterly instincts kicking in as I pull her back.

"To the bathroom," she says, struggling to rise with her bony legs.

And finally, after six years, I snap.

"To do what?" I yell, tears immediately welling. "To take more laxatives? To stick your fingers down your throat?"

"To do what I need to do," she says, her voice loud but about to break.

"What you need to do to do what, Lana?" I ask, now completely sobbing. "To turn into Mom? To make me watch over every piece of freaking food you put in your mouth to make sure you don't collapse?"

"You don't understand," she says, now crying her eyes out, too.

"No, I don't understand. Explain it to me, Lana! What is so damn awful about your life that you have to nearly kill yourself every day just to deal?"

She turns to me, an expression of pure anger. It's a look I rarely see from my sister, and this fury has never before been turned on me. I back up, afraid of what is about to come out of Lana's mouth.

"You don't get it because you're set, Morgan," she says, eyes hollow and tired. "You've got it all."

"Right," I say, my voice dripping with contempt. She is *not* pulling this card on me. "I get ignored at my own freaking *lunch table*. I don't fit anywhere, Lana. Not at school, not with my friends, and definitely not in the perfect little happy Tannunbum family. Nobody would even notice if I fell off the face of the planet. What the hell do I have that makes me "set"?"

Lana stops. "You're not planning on falling off the face of the planet, right?"

"No," I say. Other people may not want me around, but I do.

"Good," she says. She suddenly remembers she's pissed at me and raises her voice to answer my question. "You're set because you're smart and you're funny and you're a damn good writer. Who the hell else has a script under consideration by Hollywood's top teen movie director at your age?"

I don't answer. She rages on.

"You are set for life, Morgan. You're going to find a guy who loves you not for your name but who you are, and not be accountable to anyone but yourself, and be able to be whoever the hell you want to be without the public at large watching every single move you make, judging you for every freakin' thing that you do…"

Lana doesn't make it all the way through her impassioned outburst, collapsing into sobs against the foot of her bed.

I sit down next to her.

"Lana," I say. "Lana, look at me."

Her head stays firmly planted down.

"Look at me, Lana."

She obliges, slowly.

"You. Need. To. Stop. That is non-negotiable. The whole hospital incident…Lana, what if I hadn't found you? What if Ringo hadn't gone running into your room, or if I'd been 10 minutes later? What then?"

She doesn't answer. The silence hangs heavy in the air. I push on.

"You have to stop. If you can't on your own, that's ok. I'll help you find somebody who's used to dealing with this stuff and then they can help you."

"No," Lana says. "No shrinks."

"Ok," I say. "Fine. But first we're going to do two things."

"What?" she asks.

"Number one, I'm going to go downstairs and get you something to eat."

She groans, her head falling straight back into her lap.

"And number two…we're going to go shopping."

Her head shoots straight up.

"Shopping?" she says. "You *hate* shopping."

"Yeah," I say, picking up her now too-skinny double-zero jeans. "Well, you don't. Let's go get you some clothes with a real number for a size."

She reluctantly stands up, and we start to head out the door.

"Grab your wallet," I add as I pass her dresser. "I'm not *that* good of a sister."

She gives me a wary glance but also a small smile as we head out the door.

Chapter 16:

"I once had a girl/or should I say/she once had me." –The Beatles, Norwegian Wood

I spend the next two days coming up with every excuse I can to get out of the house. I still have no ideas on stalling Dad any further, and I avoid him like the plague. Thankfully, LDE practice takes a good ten hours for all the groups, and I stay the whole time, watching the freshman Choral Reading fall to pieces and laughing uproariously at Emilee as a befuddled waitress in *Almost, Maine*. Mrs. Kay doesn't say anything about me not leaving. She knows I'm just trying to avoid my family.

Eventually, I have to leave, sneaking up to my room as soon as I get home. At about 9:00, there's a knock on my door. It's not Lana and I's code, so it's either my mother or my father. Crap.

"Who is it?" I shout, with as much vocal nonchalance as I can muster.

"It's your Dad," responds my father.

My improvisation skills kick in, and I come up with a diversion.

"Just a sec," I say, making my voice sound weaker and more tired.

I jump off my bed and grab a few items, placing them just so around my room. Wrapping a blanket around myself, I head to the door.

"Yeah?" I say, opening the door just wide enough so he can see my heating pad on my bed, the Midol and glass of water on my headboard, and the "Growing Up as a Woman" book lying on the floor.

"Are you ok?" he asks, clearly falling for my staged excuse.

"Yeah," I say, clutching my stomach. "I'm just cramping and stuff and PMSing really bad and…"

He stops me. "Ok," he says. "Feel better."

He leaves. Ha. There is nothing that will make my father flee faster than the thought of a girl's menstrual cycle. Mom and Lana turn into monsters when they get their periods, and Dad has learned to run for the hills. I'm not as bad because I get mine more than twice a year (that's what eating will do for you), but there's no reason I can't use that fear to my advantage.

Knowing Dad will not come near me the rest of the night, I crawl into bed and watch TV online until midnight. I don't know if I can keep Dad away for all of tomorrow –but I can certainly try.

Turns out I won't have to keep Dad away after all. I get a text from Justin that wakes me up at the incredibly early hour of 11:00 am. Dad hasn't tried to awaken me for fear of what I may do. (When he tried to wake Lana up last time she had hers, she threw a pillow at him.)

Justin's text reads as follows: "All hands on deck @ food shelf. Huge donation and need everyone we can get. Thanx."

Perfect. I roll out of bed and start to get dressed, throwing on sweatpants and a T-shirt. Stepping outside my door, I knock on Lana's door.

"What?" Lana calls out, grumpily. Lana, like me, is not a morning person.

"Did you get Justin's text?"

"Yeah, I'm coming," she says, with a little more enthusiasm in her voice. Lana loves sorting donations.

I head off to my bathroom to quickly prepare myself for the day. A few minutes into the wrestling match between my hair and I to get it into a ponytail, Lana comes in. She's dressed in her Food Shelf Outfit again.

"Sorry," she says, as I give up on my hair and start brushing my teeth. "I couldn't find my yoga pants."

"Ith fine," I say, through my toothbrush. "I'm gwad gyou can helpf."

"What?"

I take a quick spit break.

"It's fine, I'm glad you can help."

"Oh," she says. "No problem. How are things with Dad?"

"Whath do you mean?" I say, back to scrubbing my molars.

"Is he on to you?"

"I donth really know," I say, spitting again. "I distracted him last night."

97

"How'd you do that?" she asks, impressed. Dad is not easy to fool.

"Pretended to PMS," I answer, setting my toothbrush down.

"Nice," she says, laughing. "Ready to go?"

"Yeah," I say, taking a quick gulp of water. "Let's go."

Traffic is light in Marquette on Sunday mornings, and Lana and I get to the Food Shelf after a quick fast food breakfast run for me. (She didn't get anything. Shocker!) We step inside the church and Justin is waiting for us among the massive piles of food.

"I'm so glad you guys are here," he says, heaving an audible sigh of relief. "Everybody else can't be here for another couple of hours."

I'm still in awe of all the food lining the walls. The school donation from earlier is nothing; there's barely room to walk the hallway. Pallets of corn, mixed vegetables and applesauce tower over me. This is too much food for Marquette –no doubt we'll be sending most of it to the food pantries in Compton or other nearby cities with more need than us.

"Where is this from?" Lana asks Justin, incredulously. She seems as overpowered as I am.

"I don't know," he says, shrugging. "Nobody knows, actually. Sounds like it was a donor who wished to be kept anonymous."

There's our secret benefactor again. Either Lana is giving among the best performances of her career, or it's somebody else. Hmm…

"We're going to run out of pallets," Justin says, breaking my reverie. "So I sent out some of the kids in my class to go get some."

"Some of the kids in your class?" Lana asks. I know Justin goes to UCLA, but I can't remember what he majors in…

"Public Health and Nutrition," he says. "Part of our curriculum is spending time with local grocery stores, who happen to have a ton of empty cardboard boxes lying around."

"Good thinking," I say. "So you're a nutritional science major?"

"Yeah," he says. "Guilty as charged."

Nutritional Science, huh? So someone who wouldn't let Lana get away with eating the way she does. The world needs more nutritional science majors.

"Fortunately for us," Justin continues. "Whoever donated this kept some of it sorted. This whole hallway is already in pallets by food type. There's also a ton of what we need. A good third of this is peanut butter."

Wow. Whoever did this knows our food shelf.

Justin seems to read my mind. "I know, right? I wonder who our Guardian Angel is. Wouldn't that be funny? If somebody around here was secretly a billionaire or something?"

I stifle a laugh. Justin clearly does not understand the irony of his statement. "Sounds like a TV show."

"Yeah," he says. "Well, no complaints. I don't care if it's Godzilla giving us the food, just keep it coming!"

So Justin really doesn't know who Lana is. No wonder she loves it here.

He grabs a pallet of corn and hauls it down. "Can you grab the door for me?" he asks.

"Yeah," I say, headed toward the pantry. Asking someone to get the door for you here is a task that's a little easier said than done. Outsmarting the busted lock requires stealth, talent and perfect timing.

In other words, I'm really bad at it.

This time, however, after fumbling with the rusted bolt, I manage to pull the door open, squishing myself awkwardly up against the wood while Justin squeezes by with the corn.

Shelving the cans, Justin goes back to the hallway to grab another load of food. Following his lead, Lana joins in, her puny arms barely able to handle a small box of instant meals. As she passes me, still holding the door, she grins and says, "Don't get locked in."

"Shut up," I say, but I'm smiling, too. The busted lock traps me inside the Shelf on a fairly consistent basis –probably once every three or four times we come. I have to call Lana on her phone to go get the keys and free me. She'll come to the door, jingle the keys loudly, and refuse to let me out until I agree to let her "do something about my hair".

I've had some time to think about what Lana said during our mini-fight, too, and she's kind of right –well, more right than I originally gave her credit for. I do have a lot more freedom than she has. If I want to go to the store and buy Squeeze cheese, I can buy Squeeze cheese without someone stopping me in the aisle to ask for an autograph, or snapping a picture and selling it to People magazine for the "Stars: They're Just Like Us" section. And when the guys at my school (or just the world in general) realize that I *am* a girl and therefore datable, I will have full assurance that whomever is desperate enough to ask me out is not doing so for my name.

Justin passes me with another pallet of corn, and I have an epiphany.

Justin is perfect.

Not for me. Well, maybe for me…but that's not the point. He's perfect for Lana.

Justin knows that my sister loves Minnie Mouse, hates spiders and has a particular fondness for the little kids who come in on distribution days at the Shelf. He knows she's kind, and tough, and not afraid to get her hands dirty or stick up for herself. Justin knows my sister –he just doesn't know she's a Tannunbum.

It's absolutely perfect. Lana's few dating relationships since her teens have not lasted long; the only guys that asked her out were only interested in her for two things: her name and her body. She wasn't OK with them taking advantage of either. None of them gave a crap about Lana herself. Justin would.

And I know enough about Justin to be more than ok with him going out with her. He's an Iowa boy; born and bred on a farm with the super toned muscles to prove it. He's hot –but not in a cocky, "I know I'm really sexy, so worship me" kind of way. He's polite and respectful, especially to the people who come in on distribution days, who really don't get treated well anywhere else. Plus, he's a nutritional science major, so Lana would finally have someone in her life besides me with a not totally messed up view of food. It's perfect –so how do I get him to ask her out?

As I continue ruminating about how to get them together, Justin and Lana remain totally oblivious to my plans for their courtship. They're working together to sort through a container overflowing with boxes of macaroni and cheese, laughing together over some joke I'm not in on. The way Lana looks at him, I can tell *she'd* like to date him too –it's the same look that comes across my face while looking at photos of Ryan Reynolds.

They seem to be done with the box, because they're lifting it together and bringing it towards me and the door.

Justin, who is holding the vast majority of the weight, says, "Lana, I've got this. You can let go."

Lana, who hates feeling unhelpful, replies, "No. I'll help."

"I insist," Justin counters.

"So do I," says Lana, although her skinny arms are shaking.

They've almost reached me, and I can quickly see the gigantic box is not going to fit through the doorway if I keep standing here as a human doorstop.

Justin notices this, too, and says, "Hey Morgan, you might have to go hold the edge of the door."

"Yeah," I say, quickly formulating the perfect plan in my head. I switch positions, now holding the door open from the outside instead of leaning up against it. "Here."

"Thanks," says Justin, leading the way as he and Lana head towards the back of the Shelf, where the macaroni and cheese goes.

Now all I have to do is let go.

I release my grip on the door and it slides shut, locking into place.

"Oh, shoot!" I say loudly, in my most "I totally didn't mean to do that" voice. "Sorry, guys! Is it locked?"

I know it will be.

One of them struggles with the bolt. "Yeah," says Lana.

"Sorry!" I say again, grinning. Now the two of them will have no choice but to have a private conversation.

"No problem," says Justin, through the door. "You know where the key is, right?"

"Yeah," I say. "I'll go grab that! Are you guys ok in there alone?"

Without so much as a pause, a unison "Yes!" comes out from both of them.

Morgan Tannunbum, Matchmaker.

I run as fast as I can to the church office, grabbing the key and head back to the pantry, sticking my ear against the door to see if I can hear anything. They're talking, but

101

through the thick mahogany I can't articulate what they're saying. They go on for five minutes before the talking stops all together.

What if something's wrong? I jam the key into the door and open it as fast as I can. What awaits me is not a scene from an episode of Law and Order –it's Justin and Lana locked in a simple, romantic kiss.

Unseen by Lana or Justin, I shut the door as quietly as I can.

It's a good thing they can't see me. I can't hide my grin.

Chapter 17:

"Baby says she's mine/she tells me all the time/you know she said so/I'm in love with her/and I feel fine." –The Beatles, I Feel Fine

After Justin and Lana finally come out of the food pantry, the rest of the day goes by quickly. After twenty minutes of Justin and Lana sneaking each other big grins and winks whenever they think I'm not looking, some of Justin's classmates arrive with the boxes and we get the job done by 4 in the afternoon, loading up our excess food into a truck that will be sent over to a much needier food pantry in Compton.

Unfortunately, that means I have to avoid Dad for roughly seven hours for the remainder of Sunday. Thankfully, he still thinks I have my period and won't come near me. I need to pull this excuse more often.

I spend the rest of the afternoon and evening trying to come up with a way to get Dad off my back. I've got nothing. Even watching The Colbert Report and eating Cheese-its doesn't help. By the time it gets to midnight, I've watched the twelve episodes I've missed while dealing with *Scrambled Eggs* and have eaten a good half a box. Oops. Still, for all my caloric over-indulgence, I've got zero ideas.

Struggling to keep my eyes open as Colbert signs off for the night, I shut Laverne and put her down beside my bed. Sensing his cue, Ringo runs from the door and tries to leap onto my covers. He fails miserably, his little legs no match for the gravitational pull of his gigantic midsection. Maybe I should stop feeding him Cheese-its. I lean over and pull him onto the bed. Grateful, he crawls up beside me and we both drift off to sleep.

The FDR High rumor mill is moving at a fever pitch during lunch on Monday. Two police officers came to the office this morning and pulled Erik Anderson out of class, then hauled him away in handcuffs. Even for a school near LA, this is not a typical occurrence, and now theories of what happened are being thrown out at a breakneck pace.

"He called in a bomb threat!"

"He was smoking pot in the boys' room."

"He had a knife!"

"He punched out Mr. Cabot!"

And so on and so forth. After about fifteen minutes of listening in my stall, I hear about a dozen more variations of this rumor. At this point, Erik's going to be in prison for life.

"He keyed the principal's car!"

"He spray-painted crap in the locker room."

"He hacked the computer system and used the school's credit cards!"

Ok, this one's just not true. Erik's not smart enough for something like that. This is a kid on his third try at Spanish I.

Another voice, this one sounding more confident than the others, rises above the theories to proclaim, "Guys, it's not that exciting. He did a bunch of crap and posted it online."

The bathroom audience is captivated. Clearly, this chica has the inside scoop.

"What kind of crap?" another girl asks.

"E, coke, and pretty much everything else in one night," she said.

"Sounds like the bender from hell," one girl comments.

"Yeah," says the well-informed voice. "Well, apparently he didn't feel too bad, because he posted the entire thing on Facebook."

Facebook.

I gasp, audibly. That's the answer.

The other girls in the bathroom hear my super loud gasp and fall silent.

"Who's in there?" Inside-Scoop Girl asks to the open silence.

"Oh," I say, raising the natural pitch of my voice an octave and opening the stall door. "Sorry, guys. I just, like, can't believe he'd be like, that idiotic. Did he like, make a video of himself shooting up or like, something?"

"Oh," says Inside-Scoop Girl, who, now that I can see her, I recognize as a junior cheerleader. "No, he just kept posting about how high he was on all this different crap and then topped it off by threatening Cabot."

The rest of the bathroom oohs and ahhs as Ally, the cheerleader, continues to describe Erik's escapades while I slip quietly out the door.

I forget all about my idiotic classmate and his drugs. Facebook is the answer. Facebook is how I'm going to get my dad off my back and get rid of *Scrambled Eggs*. But first, I need to make a phone call.

Slipping under the first set of stairs, I pull my phone open and call Katie, who's being homeschooled by a bunch of tutors and can almost always run to the bathroom and answer her phone.

She answers on the fourth ring.

"What's up girl?" she says. "Everything cool?"

"Yep," I say. "No emotional breakdown today. I just have a quick question."

"K, good," she responds. " 'Cuz I can only pretend to be crapping for so long."

I smile in spite of myself. I love Katie.

"Is your brother still all 'next big thing' tech-wise?"

"Yeah…" she says, obviously confused. Katie's older brother Nathan has always been obsessed with finding the latest and greatest website before it becomes super popular and investing in it. He made a killing off of Twitter.

"Is he still on Facebook?"

Katie scoffs. "Please, he ditched that months ago. Why?"

"OK, but did he delete his account or has he just not touched it?"

"I really doubt he actually got rid of it. Nathan is a digital pack rat. I'm pretty sure he hasn't even deleted his MySpace account."

I cringe. "Really?"

"Yeah," she says. " I know, right?"

Putting aside the skeletons in Nathan's social media closet, I get back to the topic at hand.

"Do you think I could…borrow his account?"

"Borrow…why would you want to do that?"

"I want to prank my dad," I say.

Katie's excitement is obvious in her voice.

"Yes!" she says, probably a little too loudly. Her Mandarin Chinese tutor might hear her. "I've rubbed off on you! Morgan Kate Tannunbum is going to prank someone! Yes. I'm so in."

"Ok, thanks," I say. Phase one of my new plan is in place.

"Look, I've got to go," she says, her volume now back to normal. "I'll call you after Ms. Zheng leaves and you get out of school. I'm so proud of you!"

I hang up with a grin.

I think this plan might work.

What's one of the first things you do after you meet someone you'll be doing business with or partnering up with in class? Simple. You go to their Facebook page and check them out. See what they like. See what they don't. See what they do on the weekends, and, if you're me, pray it doesn't involve partying or you'll be doing the entire project yourself. It's a great way to get to know people.

Or, in my case, get people to believe you're real.

I'm going to borrow Nathan's Facebook page and change the name to something boring and not suspicious, like George Parker or Anthony Martin. Then I'll friend a few random people and post a few things, mostly about the Beatles or other things loosely related to *Scrambled Eggs*. After I update his history, I'll send a letter to Avery taking credit for *Scrambled Eggs* as Boring Name Guy and rescind my permission for the rights to the screenplay, leaving Dad, Avery and anybody else unable to make the movie. Avery will at the very least Google Boring Name Guy and eventually come across Nathan's Facebook page, which, at five years old, won't look like someone just made him up out of the blue. Nathan is 10 years older than Katie –he never lived in the house next door. My dad has never met him, so he won't recognize the pictures. I'll make up a new email address and presto –an author for *Scrambled Eggs* and a reason for Dad to stop searching for me. It's perfect, especially because Nathan fits the profile Avery developed: well-educated, upper-middle-class male age 25-30.

Pulling out Laverne, I open a new Word document and begin typing up the letter I'll send to Avery in a few days, after Katie's called me with the password and I've had time to adjust Nathan's profile.

As I begin to type the sentence, "I revoke any and all rights and permissions to *Scrambled Eggs* granted to your company", I can't help but grin. I've done it. In a week or two, life will go back to normal and I can forget all about *Scrambled Eggs* and the mess it's caused.

I can't wait.

Chapter 18:

"Help/I need somebody/help/I need anybody/help" –The Beatles, Help!

Tuesday is the best day in a while for me. Katie calls with the password to Nathan's account, and although she wants me to spill all the details on what I'm doing to it, I keep mum, promising to spill my guts once this whole deal is over. Maybe I'll even take a flight out of LAX some Friday and stay the weekend in Chicago. My classes aren't bad, either –Health is just the CPR test (easy) and we spend all period in AP Geography debating the potential legality of marijuana.

Lunch is still a low point. The rest of the group has moved on to talking about a movie night they're all planning –without me. I leave the table as soon as I'm done eating, heading straight to the bathroom to play more Pac Man.

As I'm finishing up Level 10, the bathroom is mostly empty and it's about time for me to head off to class. I'm about to hit pause on my game and get up when someone else enters the bathroom. I can tell by the sound her feet are making that she's moving slowly, looking to see if anyone else is around. I silently draw my legs up onto the seat and wait to hear what happens. A few seconds later, she gags, and from the smell wafting near me, I can pretty much assume she lost her lunch.

After she flushes, she hurries quickly out of the bathroom, walking close enough to my stall that I can see her shoes.

Sparkly silver Converse.

A few weeks go by. My *Robber Bridegroom* group for speech team gets straight ones at State, as does my Improv team, and now we're both waiting to hear if we made All-State. Lana and Justin are now full-out dating, and he's even taken her out to dinner more than once. She comes home glowing, not even seeming to notice she's eaten an entire meal. I took Ringo to the vet, who put him on a strict no-people-food diet. He's crushed.

Sparkly Shoes, whoever she is, is now throwing up almost every other day. Clearly, it's not just the school food. I really should confront her about it, but I don't know what I'd say. "Oh, I don't know who you are, but you've totally got a problem, and I only know you have a problem because I'm hiding out in here every day. Oh, and I've been trying to fix the same problem in my sister and mom pretty much my whole life, and I've pretty much failed miserably, so know you're working with a pretty great track record here?" Yeah. Not happening. I have been watching the hallways for a pair of shoes like those, though, plus the few other pairs she's been wearing. The girl must have an entire closet full of different styles of Converse.

On the *Scrambled Eggs* front, I seem to be doing fairly well. The Facebook page is up and running, and I finished my cease and desist letter a few days ago. I pulled out my binder from middle school mock trial and used all the big legal terms I could find, so hopefully Avery will buy it was written by a lawyer. I went so far as to make up a law firm (Wimmer, Linn and Associates) and a lawyer (Mel Wimmer) to write on behalf of my fictional author (George Parker). I even made my own letterhead and everything.

It's been three days since I mailed out my letter, and I wake up knowing that today, Wednesday, could be interesting. We find out about All-State, Mrs. Kay announces our musical for the spring, and, most importantly, Avery will most likely receive my letter.

I nudge the still-sleeping Ringo off of me and start to roll out of bed. Grabbing one of my cuter tops and a pair of jeans out of my closet, I spend the next five minutes rummaging around for a bra in my drawers. Once I successfully locate an undergarment that actually fits (I need to go shopping. Again. I've needed to for a few months, but I'm not in enough discomfort to warrant the hell that is bra shopping with my mother.), I toss it and my other clothes on. Taking a few moments to brush my hair into something vaguely resembling a ponytail, I look in the mirror and decide it's good enough. Heading downstairs for breakfast, I pour myself a bowl of ~~Frosted Flakes~~ Wheaties and chow down. The bag is almost empty. I thought it was full not too long ago. Dad must be stress eating again. I'm so focused on getting out the door with all my homework in tow that I barely notice Lana sitting down beside me.

"Good morning," I say, smiling. "What are you doing up?" Lana doesn't usually rise from her bed till at least 10.

"Justin's mom is in town," she says, grabbing for the Wheaties box and pouring herself a generous helping. "So we're going to show her L.A."

"That's great!" I say. Then I focus in on the fact that my sister is eating breakfast. Not even a healthy breakfast. And she's not even being forced.

"Wait," I say, pointing down to her cereal. "You know that those aren't actually…"

"Yeah," she admits, a small smile forming on her lips. "Justin kind of got me hooked on them. They're kind of his favorite food."

Damn. My matchmaking skills are even better than I thought!

"Wait…" I say. "Have you been eating these every day?"

"Not every day," she says. "But a few days a week."

My sister is eating calories. Bad, unhealthy, processed sugary Tony the Tiger calories. And she doesn't care.

I think I like Justin even more now.

I drive off to school and arrive early for Pre-Calc. We've got a test. Joy.

It's not too difficult of an exam, though, and I end up having half the class to do whatever with. I pull out my notebook and doodle my way through the rest of the period.

My other classes go by rather quickly. I try not to think about All-State, or the musical, and most certainly not *Scrambled Eggs*. I try to distract myself from thinking about all the possible scenarios: the best –Yes to All-State for musical theatre and improv, Footloose for the musical and Dad utterly abandoning any and all thoughts of making *Scrambled Eggs* a movie; and the worst –No to All-State on both counts, getting stuck with a show like Cats, and Dad somehow finding out that I'm behind *Scrambled Eggs*. Plus, of course, every other scenario in between.

I entertain (well, more worry) myself through lunch this way, thinking through all the very bad or very good things that could happen in the next twelve hours. I'm so focused on all these possible scenarios that it takes me a few moments to notice there's a big ass chunk of chicken patty stuck in my throat.

And it's not coming out.

OK, don't panic. It's fine. Just cough.

So I cough. Well, I try to cough. But no sound comes out.

Don't panic. Just try again.

So I try again. And again. Nothing.

Screw not panicking.

I wrap my hands around my throat, gesturing wildly toward my friends.

Sophie, for her credit, picks up on my distress right away.

"Oh my God," she says. "Morgan, are you choking?"

My hands are around my bleeping throat and I'm turning blue, what do you bleeping think?

I settle instead for a hurried nod.

"Alright," she says. The girl is freakishly calm under pressure. "Here I come."

She quickly rises from her seat and comes straight to me, pulling me up and wrapping her arms around my stomach. I'm starting to see spots. That can't be good.

The rest of the lunch table watches in stunned silence as Sophie thrusts her looped arms into my stomach. One thrust. Nothing. Two thrust. Nothing.

I can't breathe. I can barely see. *Shit. Shit, shit, shit, shit.*

Three thrust.

Up comes the chicken and down goes me. That blasted piece of processed meat tumbles out of my mouth as I fall to the floor unconscious, my wrist smacking against the lunch table.

Chapter 19:

"Nothing's gonna change my world" –The Beatles, *Across the Universe*

I wake up to a huge crowd of blurry people staring at me.

This can't be good.

One face becomes clear out of all the haze.

"Are you ok, sweetheart?"

Oh hell, no. Mr. Marcus O'Malley just called me sweetheart. This is bad. This is very, very, *very* bad.

"What happened?" I ask, still trying to piece together the events of the last few seconds. (Minutes? I have no idea how long I've been out.)

I take a moment to inventory. I am Morgan Kate Tannunbum. I am 16 years old. I go to the Franklin Delano Roosevelt High School in Marquette, California. All right, so far it seems all systems are go.

At least, mentally. My wrist is throbbing, and my abs feel like someone punched me. Repeatedly. Did I get beat up? Because if R.J. came at me, I better have gotten in a good shot at his family jewels...

"You choked. At lunch. Where you are right now."

Oh. Ok, yeah, that sounds like a more me thing to do.

"Oh," I say. Damn, my throat hurts.

"Who gave me the Heimlich?" I ask, as quietly as I can to avoid irritating my larynx.

"Sophie," Mr. O'Malley says. Right on cue, my friend moves from the outer ring of concerned onlookers to the floor beside me.

"Good morning sunshine," she says with a grin. "Glad you're back."

"Thanks," I say, hoarsely.

"No problem," she says. "You gave us quite a scare."

"Us?" I ask, as Mr. O'Malley and a few other staff who have gathered begin to move people away from me.

"The whole table, silly. Did you hit your head on the way down?"

"No," I say, although, once I think about it, I realize I'm not actually sure. "How did you notice?"

"What do you mean, how did we notice?" she asks, bewildered. "The hand wringing and turning purple was a bit of a clue."

"No," I say. "Why where you even looking at me? You guys don't even usually acknowledge my presence."

"Sure we do," she says, taken aback. "You just don't always seem interested in what we have to say."

I don't have much time to mull this over, however, before another person joins me floorside.

"Hi, Morgan," says Mrs. Kay, concern written all over her face. "Are you ok?"

"Yeah," I say, trying to sit up a little.

She and Sophie both gently hold my shoulders down.

"Not yet," says Mr. O'Malley, coming over from his perimeter patrol. "We have to wait for Mr. Cummings."

Our health teacher doubles as an EMT for Marquette's volunteer service. Great. How bad of shape can I really be in? I feel ok. Well, other than the throbbing pain everywhere. But I've felt worse. I think. Probably.

Mrs. Kay looks at Mr. O'Malley.

"Oh, Lord," she says. "Look at her wrist, Marcus."

"Say what?" I say, lifting the arm that's throbbing more than everything else in my body.

It's a sausage-sized, hot swollen mess.

Great.

When Mr. Cummings comes, he confirms what everyone who has even glanced at my wrist has said: it's probably broken, and I need to go the E.R.

Fantastic.

So that's how I end up in the same E.R. Lana was in a few weeks ago. With Mrs. Kay. Because Mom had a business meeting and so did Dad, leaving them both unreachable. They asked me for Lana's number, too, but I lied and said it had just been changed and I didn't know it. I didn't want to interrupt her tour of L.A. with Justin and his mom. And Mrs. Kay only has one afternoon class anyway, and Mr. Rooney offered to cover for her. So know I'm in the St. Anthony's E.R. with my English teacher. Truth be told, if I had to pick an adult to be stuck in an E.R. with, it'd probably be her. Beats my blood-phobic father or faint-hearted mom. They don't do well in hospitals.

Suddenly, a phone vibrates. I pick up mine to see who's trying to reach me, but there are no new messages.

"Must be you," I say to Mrs. Kay.

She glances down at her phone and breaks out into a grin.

"Hey!" she says, excitedly. "Mrs. Wixton just emailed me All-State results!"

I sit straight up. "And…" I ask, excitedly.

"Well, we got five groups total…" she says, as she scrolls down on her phone.

"That's a tie for our record, right?" I ask.

"Yep," she says. "Ok, here's the groups. The freshman ensemble acting and reader's theater are both honorable mention…then competing All-Staters are the varsity reader's theater, the boys who did *The Producers* for musical theater and the MASS improv team." She grins at me.

"Yes!" I say. I've never made it All-State before, neither have Shawn, Alan and Seth. Not bad for a bunch of sophomores! Alan and Seth are also in *The Producers*, so they must be over the moon.

"Do they know yet?" I ask.

"Yes, I had Mrs. Wixton put it in the end-of-day announcements."

The word *announcements* reminds me of something.

"Crap!" I say. "You were going to reveal the musical today, weren't you? Oh no! The entire speech team is going to kill me for making them wait an extra day!"

"Relax," she says. "I told Mrs. Wixton to tell them that as well."

I look at her expectantly.

"It's *Guys and Dolls*," she says.

"Yes!" I declare, starting to raise my fist in celebration but stopping when my nerves start screaming. "Ow," I say, as a bit of an afterthought.

"So," Mrs. Kay says, as we're waiting to see exactly how many different places I broke my wrist in. "How's life? You know," she adds, pointing at my wrist, which has continued to swell to a pretty impressive size. "Besides that."

"Pretty good," I say. "I think I've finally got *Scrambled Eggs* dealt with."

"Oh," she says. "How, exactly?"

I am so, so tempted to spill everything: my brilliant plans, my not-so-brilliant plans, and the entire Facebook/letter scheme.

However, I keep my cool, just in case.

"That's confidential," I say. "I'll let you know the end result."

"All right," she says, with a laugh. "I trust you. How's the family?"

"Lana's actually eating, so that's good."

"How'd you manage that?"

I pause.

"Why would you think I had anything to do with her deciding that the consumption of food was a good idea?"

She smiles at me. "Trust me," she says. "I have a feeling."

"Ok…" I say. Whatever. "Actually, it's more Justin, her new boyfriend. He got her hooked on Frosted Flakes."

"Oh, so we have a new boyfriend now," she says with a grin. "Do you approve?"

"Actually," I say, before I can stop myself. "I set them up."

Mrs. Kay just grins at me, and the conversation about who is responsible for Lana's sudden appreciation for processed corn flakes comes full circle.

"See what I mean?" she says.

Damn, this woman is good.

At this moment, an M.D. in scrubs (unfortunately not Super Hot Doc) has come in to inform me that I have indeed fractured my wrist in two places. Thankfully, I won't need surgery, just eight weeks in a cast. Everything else –the sore abs and 45 seconds I blacked out –haven't resulted in a concussion or internal injuries, just the need for some Tylenol. I pick out a color for the cast –I go with purple this time, I haven't had purple yet –and a few hours later I'm good to go. Mrs. Kay drives us back to the school so I can grab my assignments and such.

I spend a few minutes fishing through my locker, searching in vain for a project rubric that seems to have tumbled out of my folder. Doing this one-handed is not an easy task, not made easier by the fact the very tiny locker seems to hold a whole lot of loose papers. It's the Bermuda Rectangle in there –that rubric is gone for good.

Giving up on the Geography grading sheet –I can always ask for a new one tomorrow; Mr. O'Malley will probably take pity on me –I turn to the next issue: my backpack. It's a huge Swiss Army bag designed to evenly bear the weight of all your crap on both shoulders. Which is great…if one of your shoulders is not in a sling.

"Guess I'll need to pull out the old messenger bag," I say, as I'm attempting to hoist the loaded down backpack onto my good shoulder.

Mrs. Kay grabs it from me. "Oh no, you don't," she says, hoisting it onto her back. The weight of the bag nearly doubles over her tiny frame.

"Dang," she says. "What do you have in here, anyway?"

"Let's see…" I say. "Most of my textbooks, folders and notebooks, plus a copy of *Scrambled Eggs*, the novels I'm reading and my middle school mock trial binder."

She gives me a quizzical glance as I mention that last item.

"It's part of the *Scrambled Eggs* plan," I explain.

"Alright," she says. "I trust you."

Just then, Sophie and Emilee come up from behind me.

"Hey!" says Sophie, twirling her keys in her hand. "You ready to roll?"

"Yep," I say, tossing Emilee my lanyard. "Thanks, guys."

Mrs. Kay turns.

"So you've got a ride home?" she asks.

"That's us!" say Sophie and Emilee in unison.

"But what about your car?" asks Mrs. Kay. "Didn't you drive?"

"We're using N.E.R.D.D.S.!" say Emilee and Sophie, again in unison and giggling.

"What?" Mrs. Kay is utterly lost.

"It's an acronym," I say. "With two D's."

"It stands for Nyquil Emergency Response Designated Driving System!" adds Emilee.

Mrs. Kay doesn't seem to be helped much by this clarification. Emilee and Sophie begin to attempt to explain the story behind the system.

"We were all at a party at Eleanor's house…"

"She lives in the middle of the woods,"

"Not like in the *middle* of the woods, but in a wooded area,"

"She does too live in the middle of the woods!"

"Ladies!" Mrs. Kay interrupts. "She lives near trees. Keep going."

"Well," continues Emilee, undaunted. "Sophie's allergies and sinus problems were really acting up."

"Yeah," nods Sophie.

"Like, *really* acting up," emphasizes Emilee. "And she already had a cold."

"So I was pretty much miserable," adds Sophie.

"Pretty much," continues Emilee. "But Eleanor's mom didn't have much cold stuff. And so she took the only cough suppressor they had."

"Which was Nyquil," I say.

"Bad idea," comments Sophie.

"Yeah," says Emilee. "Like, a really bad idea. She pretty much fell asleep right there on the spot."

"And," I jump in. "We knew it wasn't safe for Sophie to drive in that condition, but we didn't know what we going to do because she brought her car to Eleanor's."

"Which is in the middle of the woods," says Emilee.

"So it's kind of a long drive," Sophie adds.

"So we thought she was going to have to stay at Eleanor's house, but that would have been a problem because she had work early the next morning."

"So we came up with the N.E.R.D.D.S. system, which takes whoever can't be driving and two other people."

"Yeah," I say. "That's why there are three of us."

"I'll drive Morgan home in her car," says Sophie.

"And I'll follow behind in mine," adds Emilee.

"So when Morgan's home and comfortable and such," continues Sophie.

"I'll drive the two of us back to school so Sophie can get her car," finishes Emilee, with a note of pride.

"Sounds like you ladies have things under control," says Mrs. Kay, as we all start to walk toward the parking lot. "How often have you used the D.O.R.K.S. thing?"

"N.E.R.D.D.S.," Emilee says. "And only one other time."

"Kaci drove herself to the soccer regional championships but got a concussion and the P.T. people wouldn't let her drive home, which was a really good idea because…"

Just then, my phone vibrates. It's my Dad calling.

"Hi Dad," I say.

"What happened?" he asks, genuine concern in his voice. "I was with Avery all afternoon and I just got the message! What happened?"

He was with Avery all afternoon.

Oh, boy.

"Morgan…Morgan are you there?"

"Yeah," I say. "Sorry, the reception's not great in here."

I go on to explain the situation with my wrist and that Emilee and Sophie are driving me home. After he expresses his concern a few more times, he tells me he has to go deal with some legal issues and hangs up.

Sounds like tonight could be the last great battle over *Scrambled Eggs*.

Chapter 20:

"If there's anything that you want/If there's anything I can do/just call on me/and I'll send it along/with love/from me/to you." –The Beatles, From Me To You

"So how's the wrist?" Sophie asks as we pull out of the FDR High parking lot.

"It hurts a little, but not too much," I say. Truth be told, the pain meds from the E.R. are still in full effect. I don't feel a thing.

"Is that the same wrist you broke in 6th grade?"

"Yep," I say. "And 4th grade, too."

"Dang."

And awkward silence follows.

"Morgan," Sophie says, turning to me. "What is going on with you? You're not talking at lunch and you're leaving halfway through. You seem really distracted in class, and you haven't mocked Mr. Holland for writing on the divider in weeks. What's going on?"

"You notice that I leave during lunch?" I ask, dumbfounded. None of them has said a word to me about it, and we have tons of classes together.

"Of course," she says. "What are you doing, anyway?"

I look up at her.

"Playing Pac-Man," I say, quietly.

"What?"

"I'm playing Pac-Man on my phone in the bathroom."

"Why?"

"Because you guys don't seem to want me around."

"Of course we want you around!" says Sophie, looking at me. "Why would you think we didn't?"

"Because you never talk to me."

"But you never talk to us!"

"But I try, Sophie! I try to talk and you or Olivia or Kaci just talk right over me and I can never get a word in edgewise!" I say, tears rising. The fact that I'm about to cry pisses me off. What am I, a Gossip Girl? "It sucks, ok? To not feel wanted. To feel like nobody would notice if you fell off the face of the earth."

Sophie pauses for a moment.

"You're right," she says. "We are kind of loud, and I know sometimes we drown out the quieter girls at our table. And I'm sorry if I…if we ever make you feel like we don't want you around. Because we do."

She takes a deep breath and continues.

"But we do notice you, Morgan. I saw you choking today right away, and Olivia and Eleanor picked up on it right after. We all noticed you leaving halfway through lunch. It just doesn't seem like you really care what we have to say either, no offense. You're really spaced out and don't really seem to engage much. And…" she takes another deep breath. "That brings us back to 'what is going on'? Because you're really not being you."

I take a deep breath.

"I've been dealing with some…stuff, ok? It's under control and it's almost…over, I think, and…it's just been really stressful, and I can't really tell anybody about it, and…yeah."

Wow. That was like verbal food poisoning.

Sophie, for her part, is not satisfied with my answer.

"What on earth could you not tell anybody about? And how could it almost be over? And how do you know for certain it's over?"

I answer with an equally word-vomity response.

"I…I just know, ok? And it's really complicated and once it is really over, we will go get coffee and I will spill the beans, but for now…yeah. But I'm fine. Really. I've got this under control."

"Uh-uh," Sophie says, clearly not believing me as we pull onto my street.

"And, oh my God!" I say, horrified as I realize I've left out something pretty important. "Thank you! Thank you, thank you, thank you! Oh my God, you with the Heimlich and everything and…Oh, my God! It just totally hit me…Thank you!"

Sophie grins.

"All in a day's work."

"No, seriously…thank you! Oh my gosh, if you hadn't been there…"

"Then Kaci or Olivia would have done it."

"So like I said, if you hadn't been there!" I say. Olivia and particularly Kaci are not known for their proficiency in Health Class. When Mr. Cummings started to lecture on ADD, Kaci turned around and said, "Ok, so, that's like AIDS, right?"

"Seriously, though," says Sophie, the grin fading from her face. We're sitting in my driveway now, and Emilee is pulling in right behind us. "I'm glad you're ok. You really scared me for a second there, and I'm just really relieved that things worked out ok. I don't know what I'd do…" Her voice trails off.

"Awww…" I say. "Come here, girl."

She and I hug, or at least try. It's no easy task, being in a car, both wearing seatbelts and me in a sling.

"And," she continues. "We need to hang out more, ok? I know things have been rough for you with Katie leaving and everything…"

You don't know the half of it, sister.

"…and so we need to spend some quality time together."

I can't help asking.

"Vampire, werewolf, and supernatural-creature free quality time?"

"Absolutely," she says, with a grin.

We're attempting another awkward embrace when Emilee knocks on the window.

"Sorry to interrupt the love fest," she says, her smile wide as Sophie rolls down the window. "But you should get some rest."

"Yeah, it's been a long day," I say, trying to open the passenger door one-handed. It's not working.

Sophie turns off her car and pops the trunk before coming over to free me.

"Here you are, my lady," she says, with an elegant bow.

"I've got the bag," calls Emilee from the behind the car.

A few seconds later, there's an audible grunt and a few keenly timed obscenities.

"Holy crap, girl! What the hell are you lugging around in this thing?"

"Mostly textbooks and stuff."

"Well, it's freakin' heavy!"

And so we, the N.E.R.D.D.S. triple threat, shuffle toward my garage.

Maybe I have better friends than I thought.

When we step in the house, Sophie sets my bag down by the door.

"Are you sure you don't need anything?" she asks.

"Nope, I'm good."

"You're absolutely positive?" Emilee presses.

"Yes," I say. "Now leave and go get your own cars so you're not late getting home!"

"Aye-aye, captain," Emilee says. "See you around."

As they're both headed out the door, Sophie turns back.

"I was totally serious about hanging out."

"Good," I say with a smile, even though the pain meds are wearing off and my wrist is quickly starting to ache.

When the door shuts, I'm startled by the sound of Lana's voice.

"Morgan Kate Tannunbum, what did you do?"

I turn around.

"And a sling, too, really? What did you do this time?"

"Choked on a chicken patty."

"How'd you break your wrist by choking?"

"I passed out," I say. "This," I point to my cast with my good hand. "Happened on the way down."

Lana is too mad at me for not keeping her in the loop to be concerned.

"Why didn't you call? I got a message from Mom that you got hurt but were generally ok…she's still meeting with the Victoria's Secret people, by the way, she'll be home later. But why didn't you call me?"

Lana looks genuinely hurt.

"I didn't want to interrupt your romantic date with Justin."

After a brief pause, during which her eyes sparkle a little at the mention of her boyfriend, she says indignantly, "But that's no excuse! I'm your sister! I'm supposed to be here for you!"

"And you are," I say. "Just not in E.R.s. Where there tends to be blood."

"And I would have texted," I add. "But…" My voice trails off as I glance down at my busted wrist.

"Oh, you!" Lana says, in an exasperated tone. She can't hide the smile tugging at the corners of her lips, though, and she takes me by the good shoulder.

"Come on," she says. "I'll order Greg's for dinner. You," she steers me in the direction of the couch. "Are going to plop down right here and find us something good to watch."

Practically shoving me down onto the sofa, Lana hands me the remote.

"How's the pain?" she asks, plopping down next to me.

"It's ok," I say. "I've been in worse."

After a few moments of silence, I add, "I think I finally got Dad on *Scrambled Eggs*."

And so I explain the whole plan to my sister. The crappy Our Town essay, the "lost" phone message from Marshall Investigations, and of course, the grand finale: my Facebook and fake law office masterpiece.

"And," I add as I finish up the story. "I think I'll find out tonight whether or not he fell for it. He's been in meetings with Avery all day, and he told me he was dealing with 'legal issues'…"

"First off," Lana says. "I must say, I'm fairly impressed with this deception of yours. I think he'll fall for it, hook, line and sinker! But just in case he doesn't…" she says, looking straight at me. "I'm going to tell him you're exhausted tonight and not up to talking to anyone."

"What?!" I say, straightening my back and therefore my wrist. Ow. "But I want to know tonight!"

"Yeah," says Lana. "Which is totally understandable. But you're too drugged up and tired to be able to come up with an on-the-fly plan B if something goes wrong. Trust me, you'll thank me later."

If this were a normal night, I'd argue her to the death. But my wrist is really starting to hurt, and I'm getting pretty tired. It's not even 5 o'clock yet, and I know I won't be awake for much longer.

So that's why I let Lana win this argument. Because I'm tired and in pain. Not because she might be right, or anything.

Setting down her copy of "Solving America's Hunger Crisis", Lana grabs the remote from me and turns on the TV, going to the DVR to start my favorite movie in the whole world: *Mean Girls*. Lindsey Lohan has barely met Regina George when I fall fast asleep, slumping against the couch as I drift away to the sound of the ceiling fan.

Chapter 21:

"I don't care too much for money/money can't buy me love," – The Beatles, Can't Buy Me Love

Turns out I wouldn't have been able to eavesdrop on Dad anyway. Because I sleep. And sleep. And sleep. And wake up to pee. And move to my room. And sleep. And sleep. And by the time I really wake up again, it's 8:30 the next morning.

Crap.

"I'm late!" I shout. "Oh, crud, I'm late!"

Lana, who is sitting at the edge of my room holding a book, is laughing.

"Relax," she says. "Dad already called the school. They know you're coming."

"So I'm excused?"

"Yeah," Lana says. "So take your time. I didn't think you'd wake up for another few hours."

"Yeah," I respond, trying to prop myself up with only one elbow. "Well, this bear can only hibernate for so long."

"Need any help getting changed?" Lana asks.

"Oh come on," I implore. "Seriously? I've been picking out my own clothes since I was six; I think I've got this figured out. They might not be the most fashionable of outfits…"

Lana just stares at me.

"Oh," I say, looking down at my wrist, still in a sling. "No…um, no. I've got it. This isn't my first rodeo."

"OK," Lana says. "Well, be quick about it. I'm going to go put a breakfast pizza in the oven."

"We have breakfast pizza?" I ask, as I pick through my closet to find my favorite ironic T-shirt.

"We do now," says Lana, with a grin. "I went to the store and bought some last night. I snuck it in the house when Mom wasn't looking."

"Why?" I ask. "I mean, thank you, thank you, thank you; you know I love breakfast pizza and all, but…um…why?"

"Because you're hurt and I wasn't there for you," she says.

I give her a Look.

"And…" she adds, a little mischievously. "I wanted to try some. Justin swears by the stuff."

Justin is winning more and more points in my book.

After we've finished the pizza, (Lana takes off all the sausage and bacon, but she still eats a small slice), my sister heads to the living room.

"Here you go," she says, taking my messenger bag off of the couch and setting it down beside me.

I've forgotten almost completely about my need to switch bags.

"Don't bother," I say to Lana as she reaches for her keys. "Getting all my old crap out of here and switching my new stuff over might take a while."

"Look inside," Lana says, taking her keys off the rack.

I do. The bag is full of my current school supplies. Well…kind of. It looks like my folders, notebooks, textbooks and planner. Except different. There are no loose papers jammed into every open space. Extra lead and broken pencils are not falling out of every crevasse.

"I took out your middle school mock trial binder," says Lana. "I figured you didn't need that anymore."

Rifling further through the messenger bag, I see the rest of my highlighters, erasers and red pens placed in well thought-out locations, grouped by writing utensil type and color. Taking out my folders, I see each with a brand new label. Upon opening them, I see all my papers have been sorted by subject, then due date.

"It's so…organized," I say, turning to my sister. "How am I supposed to find anything?"

She laughs.

"Trust me, you'll survive. Come on, let's go."

I get to school just in time for AP Geography.

I slide into my seat right before the bell rings.

"Oh my God, so I heard what happened at lunch yesterday…" starts Sarah, who sits behind me.

"Yeah…" I say.

"So, do you remember Mr. Rooney giving you mouth-to-mouth?"

Oh hell, no.

"What?" I say. "That did *not* happen. At all. Who told you that?"

"It didn't?" Sarah asks. She almost seems disappointed. "Oh, I've heard that from like, 20 different people. So, like, who gave you mouth-to-mouth, then?"

Great. So now I've broken my wrist, passed out in front of everyone, and now rumor has it Mr. Rooney went all CPR on me. Fan-frickin'-tastic.

Sarah, not wanting to wait for my response, offers her own guess.

"So was it Mr. Cabot instead?"

"No!" I say. "The vice principal didn't either. No administrators gave me mouth-to-mouth yesterday, ok?"

"Wait…" she says. "So it was a teacher?"

Seriously?

"No!!" I say. Seriously, how dumb can this girl be?

"So it was a student…OMG, was it Jordan Erikson? 'Cuz he's a lifeguard and he's *soooo* hot…I would so let him give me CPR…"

"No!!" I say, starting to really get irritated. I can't gesture effectively one-handed, either, which is not helping my stress. "Seriously?! Mr. Rooney did not give me rescue breaths, Jordan Erikson did not give me rescue breaths, NO ONE gave me rescue breaths yesterday, is that clear?"

Unfortunately for me, most of this tirade occurs when the entire class has stopped talking…because Mr. O'Malley is standing at the front of the classroom. Staring at me.

Great.

Once the horribly awkward silence that follows passes, Mr. O'Malley steps up to the front of the class and announces that we will be starting the new project he gave us the rubric for yesterday today, and if we could please get that rubric out that would be great.

Opening the folder now neatly labeled "Human Geography Advanced Placement", I see the formerly M.I.A. rubric sitting right up front. I love Lana.

"Alright," says Mr. O'Malley. "So I've assigned the partnerships this go-around."

There is a large collective groan.

Mr. O'Malley ignores this unanimous opinion and continues, "Part of the adult world is working with people you do not know or maybe don't even like. You need to learn to cooperate with everyone, not just your friends. So, here goes: Sarah, you're with Matt; Kaci and Anna are partners, so are Nathan and Seth; Morgan, I've paired you with Seirra…"

Oh, come on. Really? Mr. O'Malley, I broke my wrist yesterday. Don't I get at least a few sympathy votes here?

When Mr. O'Malley finishes his list, Sierra comes over to my desk.

"Look," she says. "I'm not any happier about this than you are. I can't believe I got stuck with you freaking again!"

Right back at you, I think, but as I'm looking down to avoid eye contact with the she-devil, I can't help but notice her footwear.

Sparkly silver Converse sneakers.

No way.

Sierra can't be my mysterious bathroom buddy…can she?

As I'm hanging out in the bathroom at my usual post, I'm distracted, waiting for Sparkly Shoes to make her now daily entrance. Sophie didn't want me to leave the lunch table, but I told her it was a today-only deal and I had something I needed to take care of. I'm off my game in Pac-Man, too –I keep getting eaten on level 2 or 3. Now that I've seen Seirra's Converse, I have to know if she and Sparkly Shoes are one and the same. I hope she's not. Because that would mean feeling bad for her. Which I don't want to do. But I would anyway. And I don't want to feel sorry for her. Because she's mean. And she thinks she's better than everyone. But I wouldn't be able to feel nearly as guilt-free putting her pink, fluffy ego in place if I knew she was dealing with…this. Because this sucks.

While the proverbial devil and angel on my shoulders are fighting it out over whether Sierra is a soulless Queen Bee or a little girl lost, Miss Sparkly Shoes herself makes an entrance. I hold my breath. I don't want to open the door until after she goes into the stall and does her thing; I want to be sure I have the right Sparkly Shoes instead of a wrong-place, wrong-time trend follower. Sure enough, a few seconds later comes the always attractive sound of someone forcing their food back up. As quietly as I can, I open the door to my hideout stall and go to the sinks, nonchalantly turning on the water –not a simple task one-handed. As I'm struggling with the hot water knob, Sparkly Shoes opens up her stall and runs out of the bathroom, trying to hide her face from me.

It doesn't work. It's Sierra, plain as day.

Darn.

I know what I have to do. As much I dislike Sierra, I can't ignore my conscience. I'll drop a quick, anonymous note in the guidance office's drop box. I won't leave my name, just hers and a quick overview of the situation.

But I won't just do that. I'll get to her tomorrow, corner her in the bathroom so she can't run away from me. I'll tell her I know about the purging and I won't tell anyone (and I really won't; I'm not sinking to her level of Queen Bee evilness), but I'm here if she needs to talk because I kind of know what she's going through, at least by proxy, anyway.

I know this is the right thing to do, but I'm not looking forward to it. If she knows I'm the one who told the counselors, I'm screwed. If one part of my own mini-intervention goes wrong, I'm screwed. But she already despises me anyway, so what have I got to lose? Besides, to be honest, what I really hate about this plan is that it involves me talking with her. When I don't have to be. And offering to talk to her more, if she wants. Which, she probably won't, but still, the thought of more conversations with Sierra Solomon makes *me* want to hurl.

Stupid conscience.

Chapter 22:

"Come on/come on/shake it up baby now/shake it up baby" –The Beatles, Twist and Shout

I deal with the FDR High grapevine the rest of the day. There are dozens of variations on what really happened yesterday, most of which involve me looking even stupider than I already did. One rumor has me suing the school over the consistency of the chicken patty I choked on, while another has one of the seniors, Mark Matheson, giving me the Heimlich and carrying me out of the lunchroom to the nurse's office Snow White style after I passed out. (*That* I would not have minded. That boy is H-O-T. Dumb as a bag of rocks and a total player, but H-O-T.)

After school, I head to the guidance office and quickly drop off the brief note about Sierra I wrote between periods. But it turns out I won't have to wait for lunch tomorrow to initiate the second half of my plan. Because on my way out the door to meet Lana, I run into none other than Sparkly Shoes herself.

So I take a deep breath and I talk. I tell her I know about her throwing up every day after lunch and I won't tell anyone, but I'm here to talk if she wants.

And she responds. I won't tell you about the rest of the conversation –that's between her and me and the janitor who happened to be mopping the hallway nearby. I know she won't be halting her after-lunch ritual anytime soon (If Lana has taught me anything, it's that it has to be Seirra's choice to stop), at least maybe I've made her think about it.   And that's really all I can do, anyway.

Now hopefully she doesn't hate me more.

I walk out to the car, where Lana's waiting.

"Hey," she says. "I'm just going to drop you off at home. Justin just texted; they need my help at the Shelf."

"I'm in!" I say, climbing into shotgun after throwing my bag into the back seat.

"Um…" Lana says, looking down at my wrist.

"Oh…" I say. "Yeah…I guess this sort of limits my helpfulness, doesn't it?"

"Yeah," Lana says. "But Justin and I can handle it."

When she says the name of her boyfriend, her eyes twinkle a little.

"Oh my gosh," I admonish her. How are they this adorable after only a month? "But I don't think I could have helped out anyway. I have make-up homework from yesterday."

And a crap-ton of it at that. I missed the start of a new project and a 10 page essay on Marie Curie. Which is going to be tough to type. You know, one-handed.

At least I've got my mad handwriting skills in my corner. I've broken, dislocated, and sprained so many different parts of my right and left arms that I've learned how to write legibly with both. At this point, I'm full-out ambidextrous. So even though my right wrist is out of commission for the time being, I'll still be able to do my math and other homework that requires actually writing stuff out by hand.

There's no need to point that out to my teachers, though, right?

The typing, however, might be an issue. When I talked to Mrs. Holkum about it, she gave me the following advice:

"Have your Mom or Dad type while you tell them what to write."

Uh-huh. Not happening.

I'll figure something out. So long as it doesn't involve my mother and especially my father being anywhere near Laverne, I'll do pretty much anything.

Speaking of my father, tonight very well might be the night. Of course, if he really did fall for my letter, it's not like he's just going to announce to the entire family that the script he was in love with didn't pan out. He has to give up on scripts all the time; it's hardly a newsworthy event in our house. Finding out that he doesn't know is actually going to be harder than finding out that he does –which he hopefully doesn't. Because that would be really, really bad.

I've been trying to avoid thinking about it all day –and, thanks to Sierra, I've been pretty successful. But now, on the drive home, it's quickly consuming my brain. Two months of planning, dodging and praying come down to this.

We're almost home now. OK, Morgan, just breathe. You will be fine. He doesn't know. Just act natural and this whole thing will be nothing but a bad memory.

Lana pulls in the driveway. I slowly climb out, grab my bag from the back seat of my sister's SUV and trudge toward the house.

Prolonging the process of actually getting to the house for as long as I can without arousing suspicion, I decide I'd better go in before Dad gets suspicious. His car is in the garage. Gulp.

It's OK. You can do this. Just act natural.

I step inside the house to music playing. I recognize the band instantly –who put the Beatles on?

"Hey," says Dad, coming in right on cue. "How was school?"

"Fine," I say. So much for avoiding him. The more time I spend with him, the more likely I let something slip and the whole plan falls apart. "Um…what's with the music?"

"Oh," he answers. "I was in the mood for some Lennon and McCartney. Why? Is it bothering you?"

"No," I say. "It's fine."

"Good," he declares. "I made a playlist."

The song switches from "A Hard Day's Night" to "Yesterday" as my Dad heads back into the kitchen.

"Oh," he says, popping his head back out. "It's family dinner again tonight."

"No!" I whine. I can be honest about my loathing of Tannunbum Together Time, Dad doesn't like it either.

"Relax," he says. "I'm in charge."

OK, good. Usually Dad being in charge means Mom won't be home for dinner, which means ordering in Greg's.

"Is Mom still in designing negotiations with the Victoria's Secret people?" I ask.

"Yeah," he answers. "But she'll be home for supper."

So pizza won't fly. Bummer.

"OK," I say. "So what are we having?"

"Scrambled eggs."

"What?!"

My heart plummets, and I break out in a sweat.

He's talking about the food.

Stop panicking.

132

It's ok.

Be calm.

He's talking about the food. Right?

"What?" my Dad asks, seeming surprised to see my rather loud reaction to his choice of main course.

"I mean," I say, improv skills kicking in. "Scrambled eggs aren't very healthy. Mom won't be ok with it!"

"I'll tell her I used the egg substitute stuff and fat free cheese, free range meat, and responsibly fried bacon."

"Will you actually be using any of that?" I can't help but ask.

"Of course not!"

I'm still sweating. The Flight or Fight response we talked about in Health class is now in full effect. I want to run away as fast as I can.

I settle for heading up to my room. Dragging my bag along with, I go upstairs and open my door. I shut the door quickly but quietly and lean up against it.

AHHHHHHHHHHHHHHHHHHHHH!!!

OK, Morgan, you're just being paranoid. It's ok. It's fine. Stop being so suspicious of everything. It's just a coincidence your dad is listening to one of the most famous bands in the world and is making a very common main dish for supper.

It's just a coincidence –right?

OK, just stop. Stop panicking.

Ringo comes up to me for his daily petting. I stroke him absent-mindfully. Every ounce of energy I have is going towards not running out of the house screaming like a banshee.

Downstairs, the song switches to "Dear Prudence". Why do all these songs seem connected in my brain? I think through it for a minute. They're all from different albums, in different years, with different people on lead vocal. They were all written by Lennon-McCartney, but that doesn't mean much; pretty much every Beatles song was written by Lennon-McCartney.

While I'm musing, the song downstairs changes again, this time to "All You Need Is Love".

No way.

I fire up Laverne and open up the file to *Scrambled Eggs*. Going to the "Search" application in my word processor, I type in all four songs and get four results.

They're all songs I referenced in *Scrambled Eggs*.

Not only that, but they're in order.

OK, but I referenced a lot of Beatles songs, right? It's not weird at all that they're in order, or anything. That could totally be a coincidence.

But remembering the probability calculations we did in Math 3, I know the odds of getting 4 in the exact right order aren't really that great. But it could happen. Right?

Suddenly, my phone vibrates. The sound makes me jump.

Telling myself yet again to calm down and get a grip, I pick up my phone. I have a new text from Mom.

"meeting going pretty l8…probs wont be home 4 supper. Eat w/o me. xoxo Mom"

Apparently Dad got the same text, because a few seconds later he yells up to me, "Morgan! Your mom says she won't be home for supper! Lana too…sounds like it's just the two of us."

AHHHHHHHH!!!

Doing everything in my power to keep my voice from shaking, I yell down as nonchalantly as I can, "So I've heard. Can we order Greg's?"

"I already started mine," comes the reply. "So probably not. Sorry!"

"It's fine!" I yell back. "Call when you need me. I've got homework."

Oh my God. Oh my God. OhmyGodOhmyGodOhmyGod.

I'm in full out panic mode. What do I do? I can't take much more of this!

I'd be a terrible spy.

For the next ten minutes, I do nothing but sit on my bed and take slow, deep breaths. Ringo, sensing my distress, hops up next to me and lays his head in my lap.

I can get out of this. Odds are Dad has no clue and I'm just so scared and paranoid I'm just imagining everything has to do with *Scrambled Eggs*. All I have to do is fake it through this one family dinner and I'm home free.

Speaking of which, Dad yells for me to come down.

OK. Here we go. Be calm.

I head downstairs. Two places are set, mine and his. But he's not sitting down. He's over at the fireplace mantel…dusting the awards?

"What are you doing?" I ask. Dad doesn't dust. Well, let me rephrase. Dad doesn't dust unless Mom is making him dust. And she's not here.

"Oh," he says. "I'm just appreciating the view. Sometimes I think I forget about how great a fireplace mantel we have until someone devotes an entire monologue to how wonderful it is."

The fireplace mantel.

He knows.

He's got to know.

Right?

He wouldn't be messing with me like this if he didn't…right? But I can't say anything. Because what if he doesn't? I can't say anything unless I'm absolutely sure he knows.

Abandoning his Swiffer on the mantel, he comes to the table and sits down. Following his lead, I take my seat.

I'm sweating up a storm. It's all I can do not to hyperventilate.

Dad doesn't seem to share my anxiety. He's plugging away at his plate full of scrambled eggs, bacon, and cheese.

He takes a moment to stop chewing and points at my plate.

"Dig in," he says. "There's like a half cup of cheese in there."

Normally, the idea of this much cheese in a single dish would make my heart soar. But right now I'm so scared he'll figure out it's me I'm not even hungry.

Wow. I'm not hungry. That's a first.

Dad pauses his chowfest and second time and looks me straight in the eye.

"Would you mind getting me the ketchup, Meagan?"

Chapter 23:

"And in the end/the love you take/is equal to the love you make." –The Beatles, The End

"You bastard!" I say, before I can help myself.

My dad is laughing hysterically.

"You should have seen your face when I told you we were eating scrambled eggs," he says with a grin.

"How long have you known?" I say, bewildered. "And that was not funny!"

"Yeah it was," he says, still grinning. Turd.

I can't help it. Now I'm smiling, too.

"And," he continues. "I first suspected after I read about the Richie/Fonzie laptop-printer duo. You're the only person I know who names their electronics. And I don't know many writers that would have given a 16-year-old credit for knowing their sappy, syrupy hit comedies of the seventies."

"What I don't understand," he says "And what kept me doubting for a long time was why you were so determined to hide the fact that you wrote it from me. If you sent it in, why were you so hell-bent on keeping it from me?"

"I didn't send it in!" I exclaim. "Lana did!"

"Lana?" he asks, surprised. "Well, that explains a lot. Why?"

"She's convinced I'm the next…you!" I say, exasperated. "I haven't the slightest idea why."

"Oh, I do," Dad says. "It's very good. It's a little rough around the edges –all scripts are –but it's actually quite impressive. Why don't you want me to make it a movie? And nice work, by the way, with the fake letter. I almost fell for it."

"I didn't want you to make it a movie because I didn't want you to know I wrote it," I say, casting my eyes down.

"Why not?" he says. "It's good!"

"Why not?" I ask. "You've read it, right? I'm horrible to you guys in there! I practically rip all three of you to shreds!"

"First off," he says. "You don't rip Lana to shreds. You're just honest about…the way that she is. You're actually quite kind to her. As for me and your mother…"

He pauses. I cringe. I deserve whatever comes out of his mouth, and I know it.

"It's not the most flattering portrait of either of us," he says. "And when I first realized it was you, I was pretty angry. This whole time I've been thinking you wrote this and sent it to me with the intention to make me feel guilty for…um…the lackluster parenting I've done in the past few years. But you didn't send it in."

I shake my head.

He lowers his voice.

"Nobody was supposed to see this, were they?"

"No," I say, voice trembling. Tears are forming in my eyes. "I printed off one copy, and I gave it to Mrs. Kay."

"Your English teacher?"

"Last year, yeah," I nod. "But nobody else was supposed to see it, I swear! I accidently left it in Lana's car and she read it and hacked Laverne and emailed it to Avery."

"And I'm sorry!" I blurt out. "I'm sorry I wasn't very nice to you or Mom and I want you to know I wrote it when I was mad, ok? I was really pissed off and I just exploded. And I'm really sorry I let it get like this, where we don't even talk anymore, let alone have Morgan-Dad movie nights. And…it sucks, ok? I shouldn't have just let go of you when you got so busy because now the only reason we're talking is because I wrote a story about how horrible you are!"

I'm full-out crying now. Tears are running down my cheeks as Dad pipes up.

"You need to explode more often," he says. "Because that's a pretty damn impressive manuscript."

"And I'm sorry, too," he adds, swallowing hard and looking me straight in the eyes. "With Lana and your Mom and I really seeing all those offers happen at the same time, I'm afraid…you drew the short straw. And that's not ok. And I rationalized that you were ok on your own because you were, because you're more independent than your mom or sister and can handle a lot more by yourself. But that's no excuse for…letting the distance between us get so huge. I'm sorry I haven't really been…involved in the past couple years and I know…I deserve a lot of the potshots you took at me in there. And that's what made me the most angry –that you were more right than wrong."

We both take a deep breath.

That was probably our first real conversation since I've been a teenager.

"And so," Dad says, rising from the table. "We're going to do better. Both of us. I sort of anticipated having this conversation," he walks into the kitchen and returns with a carton of cookie dough ice cream. "And so I came prepared. So you and I," he says, going back to the kitchen and returning once more with two bowls, two spoons, an ice cream scooper and a box of tissues. "Are going to work out the rights to *Scrambled Eggs*. And then we're going to watch a movie. Your pick. You can even choose a chick-flick, if you want."

This last part moves me. Chick-flicks are the bane of my father's existence. He hates them with a burning passion, and he's willing to sit through one. For me.

"Wait," I say. "You want to make *Scrambled Eggs* into a movie, still?"

"Of course," he says. "Like I said, it needs a little editing, and we probably won't be able to get rights to the Beatles songs, but I'm still game. Why, do you not want me to?"

"I don't really know," I say, and I really don't. "This whole time, I've been so wrapped up in making sure you didn't find out I wrote it that I didn't even think about the possibility of it actually being a movie. I didn't think it was even close to good enough for that."

"Well," he says. "I'll help you with the rewrites, but yeah, both myself and Shark Studios are interested in making *Scrambled Eggs* a movie. All we need is the author's permission." He turns to me.

"But," he adds quickly. "I know –or at least, I know *now* –that *Scrambled Eggs* wasn't supposed to ever leave Shirley…"

"Laverne," I correct.

"Right," he says. "And so if you don't want *Scrambled Eggs* to ever see the light of day again, I will tell Avery all bets are off and we will forget this ever happened, ok? So, it's your call."

"Um…" I say. "Can I think about it first?"

"Absolutely," he says. "Take your time and decide. I'm totally fine with whatever you choose. Now," he turns his attention to the ice cream. "How many scoops?"

"Five," I say. I'm hungry now. "And…um…what happens if it does become a movie, like everything that has to happen…happens and it becomes an honest-to-God, in-the-movie theater movie?"

"Then it becomes an in-the-movie theater movie," Dad says. "And you'll get a screenwriting credit."

"OK," I say. The idea of something I've written opening in theaters across America is mind-blowing. I can't seem to wrap my head around it.

Dad laughs, quietly.

"You look like me the first time I was offered a writing-directing gig," he says. "Although, you're a lot younger and probably smarter."

I smile faintly.

"But," he says. "Let's focus on something else for the rest of the night, ok?" He finishes scooping himself a massive bowl of ice cream and heads over to the couch. Plopping down on the sofa, I sit down beside him after grabbing a blanket.

Clicking on the TV, Dad hands me the remote and I pick out a movie –not a chick flick but a classic from Morgan-Dad movie nights of the past: The Sting.

As the movie starts, Dad wraps his extra arm around me.

Maybe there's hope for us after all.

Epilogue:

"The long and winding road..." –The Beatles, *The Long and Winding Road*

I stroll through the aisles, searching for seat 8-C.

After a few minutes of lugging my very heavy carry-on, I find 8-C. There's no one else seated in my row yet, so I don't have to walk past anyone. I push my bag under my seat and plop myself down in the plushy cushions, pulling out my iPod and starting my Beatles playlist.

8-C is a window seat, and although the image of the tarmac isn't all that exciting, I know the view will get a whole lot better once we're up in the air.

It's been six months since that first Morgan-Dad movie night. I did ultimately decide to let Dad make the movie, and production starts in about a month. Something I hadn't considered when I first debated whether or not to let Dad make the movie was money –and it turns out the writer of the screenplay gets a lot of it. Dad made me put 80% of it in my savings account for when I go to college in a few years, but he told me I could do whatever I want with the last 20%.

So I bought a roundtrip 1st-class plane ticket, a cute set of matching luggage, and a two week supply of Cheese-its. Because I'm off to spend 14 days with Katie in Chicago at her place. I've been counting down the days before I leave for 4 months now, and now the time has finally come for me to head out. I can't wait.

My phone buzzes. It's Dad. Again. He's very concerned that I'm taking my first solo flight, although I've been texting him every five minutes like he's requested. He wanted to send Lana with me, but she had a conflict. She's in Washington, D.C., working as the celebrity ambassador for the No Child Hungry campaign. She gets to work with food pantries and kids and use her celebrity status for a cause she cares about. She's over the moon.

Her new job alone didn't send her completely over the moon, though. Justin's invitation for her to join him at his family reunion in Iowa did. She met his family, and they love her. She seems to love them back.

Things seem better for Lana than they did a year ago. She still freaks out about food every once and a while: she pulled a stunt where she didn't eat for two days when someone made a degrading comment about her weight gain; Justin and I had to blackmail her into eating by threatening to take her to the hospital. But the point is, she did gain weight, and for the most part, she's kept it on. She's definitely not "fixed" –I don't think that's how these things work. Maybe with me and Justin around she'll be just fixed enough.

As for Dad and I, we're getting along better, too. We've survived two bouts of creative differences over *Scrambled Eggs*, three Tannunbum family dinners and the remake of *Footloose*, so I'd say were doing as well as can be expected. We have a standing date every other Saturday night –movie (whose choice alternates from week to week) and an unhealthy snack (chosen by the person who didn't choose the movie). I'll be missing one such date while I'm in Chicago, I can say with full honesty I'm going to miss it.

The flight attendant, impossibly and impressively perky at this hour, begins her speech on safety and what to do in case of emergency. I pull out my earphones and buckle my seat.

I, for one, am ready for take-off.

Acknowledgements:

Here comes the part of the book that only the people who actually know the author care about. Everybody ready?

First and foremost, my parents. Thanks Dad for having me write this in the first place and Mom for raising me to read and love literature. Sorry about the library fines.

Second off, endless thanks to the teachers that put up with me and transformed an eager preteen with a passion for words into a near-adult that managed to write an entire novel. I could go through my middle and high school years and name twenty of you who have challenged and changed the way I look at myself, my classroom and my community. Each one of you has impacted me much farther than you'll ever know. Special thanks to Melissa Wimmer for all the edits and guidance from the first draft to final copy.

Thanks also to the real Karli, Em, Eleanor and Rebecca, plus Livia, Hannah, Gracia, Heidi and the gang at Journey Youth Ministries–thank you for putting up with me and Morgan from when I started this sophomore year till now. You have given me the love and support Morgan spends most of the book longing for. Y'all are the best!

And my DBFF Miss Katie McDaniel –there's a reason Morgan calls Katie in her deepest moments of crisis. You have always been there for the moments when I feel like I can't handle Type One any longer. From the memes to the surprise care packages and the Skittles and the endless Eeyore references, I can't tell you enough how much you mean to me.

My WFP friends Sean, Tariro and Dominique –our geography may still be far, but I hope our hearts forever remain this close.

And finally to Mrs. Regina Linn. I could not have done this without you. Mrs. Kay was the first character I created beyond Morgan, because I needed her to have an anchor. I've found mine in you. You have made me a better writer and human being, pushed me to new heights and taught me the value in valuing myself. I am forever grateful.